JOHN BOYNTON PRIESTLEY was born in 1894 in Yorkshire, the son of a schoolmaster. After leaving Belle Vue School when he was 16, he worked in a wool office but was already by this time determined to become a writer. He volunteered for the army in 1914 during the First World War and served five years; on his return home, he attended university and wrote articles for the *Yorkshire Observer*. After graduating, he established himself in London, writing essays, reviews, and other nonfiction, and publishing several miscellaneous volumes. In 1927 his first two novels appeared, *Adam in Moonshine* and *Benighted*, which was the basis for James Whale's film *The Old Dark House* (1932). In 1929 Priestley scored his first major critical success as a novelist, winning the James Tait Black Memorial Prize for *The Good Companions*. *Angel Pavement* (1930) followed and was also extremely well received. Throughout the next several decades, Priestley published numerous novels, many of them very popular and successful, including *Bright Day* (1946) and *Lost Empires* (1965), and was also a prolific and highly regarded playwright.

Priestley died in 1984, and though his plays have continued to be published and performed since his death, much of his fiction has unfortunately fallen into obscurity. Valancourt Books is in the process of reprinting many of J. B. Priestley's best works of fiction with the aim of allowing a new generation of readers to discover this unjustly neglected author's books.

LEE HANSON is a writer, editor, and teacher. He is the editor of the *Rediscovering Priestley* series for Great Northern Books and is also Chairman of the J. B. Priestley Society. For more information about J. B. Priestley's life and work or to join and become involved with the society please visit the official website of the estate of J. B. Priestley, www.jbpriestley.co.uk or the website of the J. B. Priestley Society, www.jbpriestleysociety.com.

Cover: The cover is a reproduction of the original jacket art from the 1961 Heinemann first edition, illustrated by John Cooper. Reproduced by permission of Random House.

FICTION BY J. B. PRIESTLEY

* Available from Valancourt Books

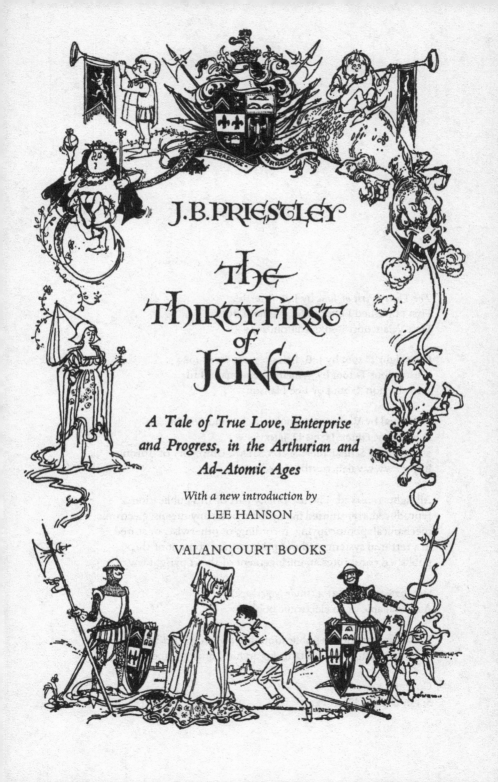

J.B. PRIESTLEY

The Thirty-First of June

*A Tale of True Love, Enterprise
and Progress, in the Arthurian and
Ad-Atomic Ages*

With a new introduction by
LEE HANSON

VALANCOURT BOOKS

The Thirty-First of June by J. B. Priestley
First published London: Heinemann, 1961
First Valancourt Books edition, 2014

Published by Valancourt Books, Richmond, Virginia
Publisher & Editor: JAMES D. JENKINS
20th Century Series Editor: SIMON STERN, University of Toronto
http://www.valancourtbooks.com

ISBN 978-1-941147-21-4 (*trade paperback*)
Also available as an electronic book.

All Valancourt Books publications are printed on acid free paper
that meets all ANSI standards for archival quality paper.

Cover by John Cooper
Set in Dante MT 11/13.2

INTRODUCTION

When *The Thirty-First of June* was published in 1961 (Priestley's 23rd novel in his 67th year) few readers would be aware that this latest book began life not as a novel but as a playscript back in 1957. There is little reason why they should, as the play never prospered, was staged only once at The Old Theatre within the unlikely venue of the London School of Economics and remained unpublished until 2013 when it was released by Oberon Books along with *Jenny Villiers*, another play that became a novel. The script's lack of commercial prospects may be attributable to the technical difficulty of staging it; it reveals no less than sixteen scene changes to accommodate numerous shifts in time and place. Priestley must have realised this soon after its only performance and his better judgement was confirmed by the book's success at the play's expense.

When asked by an audience of lecturers at the University and Institute of Foreign Literature in Tashkent (now the capital of Uzbekistan) why he had written *The Thirty-First of June* Priestley's hesitant response was, 'for fun'. What had begun as a solemn discussion of the book's significance descended at once into roars of laughter and applause. There is a temptation to think that Priestley was being glib with the assembled academics, but his words were spoken with candour, for Priestley, like Dickens, Smollett and Cervantes (three of his favourite authors) had an essentially comic view of life. Four years of front line service in the Great War and the loss of most of his friends served up enough of the tragic for him and he never allowed himself to become a writer who recycled these appalling experiences into philosophical conversations, introversion and brooding self-examination. Few, if any, of his novels or plays contain any genuine terror or real blood spilled. Even in thought-provoking works such as *Angel Pavement*, *Bright Day*, *The Linden Tree* or *Time and the Conways*, he cannot be entirely serious; humour is always allowed to poke its head up. His great friend Diana Collins once said of him: 'I've never heard Jack say anything really unkind about anybody. He can't bear human pain

and he'd never inflict pain . . . Jack's really no good at villains. He
does believe there's an active principle of evil in the world, and
yet he can't bear to create a really evil character.' This is the case
with *The Thirty-First of June*: it is a book where we find Priestley
unashamedly having fun, both with the characters and with the
reader. This is not to say, however, that fantasy and comic fiction
is superficial or trite. It is true that ordinary readers enjoy it and
few are against it, yet it is equally the case that critics often scorn
it and few major literary prizes take notice of it. It is too often
regarded as relentlessly middlebrow and its writers dismissed
merely as entertainers. This is reductionist, for as any writer or
actor who attempts it will tell you, comedy is a serious business. If
it wasn't, Cervantes would not have spent so many years shaping
Don Quixote, Thackeray would never have started *The Rose and the
Ring*, and Dickens would have left Sam Weller and Mr Pickwick to
themselves.

In *The Thirty-First of June* Priestley sets about mocking the modern world through Sam Penty, a seemingly talented artist obliged
to earn a living creating pictures for vacuous advertising projects
such as Damosel Synthetic Stockings. Sam produces for his advertising agency (Wallaby, Dimmock, Paley and Tooks) a painting of
a beautiful princess who shall beguile the female consumer into
buying the delicate tights. Meanwhile, in Arthurian England, the
beautiful Princess Melicent of Peradore, attempting to catch sight
of her own true love in a magic mirror, catches instead a glimpse
of Sam and his painting. It's love at first sight and what follows is
mayhem as the two worlds cross over and intermingle. Ad-men
find themselves in the court of King Meliot; princesses become
stars on daytime television; enchanters and a dwarf invade the Private Bar of the Black Horse Public House; and poor old Sam Penty
is forced to take on the infamous Red Knight and a fiery dragon to
win Melicent's hand in marriage. In the end the two time zones
merge so there is no longer any 'then' or 'now' and the characters
exist together in a four-dimensional state; a theme that harks back
to elements of Priestley's famous 'time plays', the serialism of J. W.
Dunne and esoteric thought of P. D. Ouspensky.

Lighter than many of Priestley's other novels it is technically
adroit, colourfully imagined, funny, farcical and has an astute eye

for satirical opportunity. The world of advertising, and the narcissistic image-conscious world it inhabits are lampooned, offering us a taste of what was to come in the riotous yet harsher satire of *The Image Men* (1968). *The Thirty-First of June* acclaims and celebrates what is important in life and pokes fun at what is not. The mythical spirit of the book is ultimately more Falstaff than King Arthur and we might conclude, as Priestley did of Falstaff and The Boar's Head Tavern, that it 'belongs to some haunting dream, perhaps as old as drink and firelight, of a gigantic wonderful night out, a hell of a party'. We know at once it is ridiculous, but can see that it comes from the same realm as those certain magical moments we all too fleetingly experience yet yearn to revisit; Priestley understood, better than most, that what drives and sustains us are their memory and our unwavering hope that the magic will come again . . .

Lee Hanson
Yorkshire, England

May 27, 2014

THE THIRTY-FIRST OF JUNE

For my six granddaughters:
Sadie Wykeham
Vicky, Karen and Sophie Goaman
Kristin and Miriam Littlewood
in the hope that a few copies of
this tale will still be around
when they all feel ready to
tackle it

Contents

CHAPTER ONE

Princess Melicent and the Magic Mirror

Lunaday, the 31st of June, brought to Peradore the kind of summer morning we all remember from years ago but seem to have missed ever since. The tiny kingdom, one of several owing allegiance to the high king Arthur at Camelot, came yawning to life in the smoky gold of that morning. Owing to the deplorable lack of progress in Arthurian England, it was all very peaceful: no old buildings were being knocked down to make room for office blocks, no take-over bids were being made, no traffic problems were giving the subjects of King Meliot ulcers or nervous breakdowns, and no office workers were packing themselves into trains that ran under the ground. Not having yet discovered economics, Peradore was not planning desperately how to make its exports exceed its imports. It was not in fact planning anything except what to have for dinner.

The West Tower of King Meliot's castle was occupied by his daughter and only child, Princess Melicent, her two damsels-in-waiting, and their maids. In the main apartment, the Tapestry Room, the musician in attendance, a young man called Lamison, was idly plucking at his lute. He was one of those thin, dark, haughty young men who are conceited without having anything to be conceited about, for he was not even a moderately good lute-player. His strumming was interrupted by the arrival of the two damsels-in-waiting, Lady Ninette and Mistress Alison.

Ninette had dark auburn hair, green eyes, a fine shape and a nasty temper. Alison was smaller and softer, a pretty mousy girl, a type that has never been in short supply in England

5

from King Arthur's day to this. Though it was still early, both girls were already feeling bored, so that Ninette looked sultry and cross and Alison damp and wistful.

Ninette immediately took it out of Lamison. 'Oh – do stop playing that boring old tune,' she told him. 'Don't you know anything else?'

Alison was reproachful. 'You promised to learn "The Black Knight Hath My Heart".'

Lamison muttered something inaudible, stopped playing, but stayed where he was, waiting for the arrival of Princess Melicent. The two girls now ignored him, stood close together, and began whispering and hissing at each other.

'If Melicent brings that magic mirror with her,' said Ninette, 'I'll ask to look into it.'

'Oh – Ninette – dare you?'

'Certainly. Anyhow, it isn't hers, and it'll have to go back to that enchanter very soon – perhaps this morning. And if she's seen somebody in it, why shouldn't I?'

'Tapestry again, I suppose,' Alison sighed. 'And I'll have a headache. Why doesn't anything happen now, here in Peradore? My cousin Elaine's having a marvellous time in Camelot. Several fascinating enchanters, two giants and a dragon in the neighbourhood, three or four castles under spells, and Knights of the Round Table all over the place, rescuing everybody – lovely parties every night.' She sighed again.

Ninette made a snorting noise. 'It's no use sighing and mooning. We must *make* things happen.'

Alison was wistful. 'You can't if you're a virtuous-damsel character like me.'

'Well, I'm *wicked* – thank goodness!' said Ninette, her green eyes gleaming. 'Let me have half a chance – and I'll make things happen. You'll see.'

Princess Melicent came hurrying in, still rubbing with a small piece of silk the magic mirror, which was about eighteen inches square, made of shining metal, and enclosed

within a dark wood frame. She had golden hair and large grey
eyes and was altogether an exquisite girl. But this morning
she had lost her usual sleepy and smiling serenity, and was
almost scowling.

'I'm *furious*,' she announced. 'I've stared and stared but I
can't see him this morning. And I'm sure he's still thinking
about me. I *feel* he is. The magic can't be working.'

'Perhaps if I had a try . . .' Ninette began.

'Certainly not. Master Malgrim, the enchanter, only lent it
to me.' She now noticed the musician. 'You may go, Lamison.
No music this morning. We're not in the mood.' She waited

until he had gone. 'It's maddening not to be able to see him again. What day is it?'

'Lunaday, the thirty-first of June,' said Alison. 'Lovely day too. Can't we go out?'

'No, my father wishes to speak to me. It'll have to be tapestry.'

Ninette made a face at Alison. 'Oh – not yet, Melicent, please. You know, you never told us what this knight you saw was wearing.'

'Well,' the Princess began, cosy and confidential at once, 'he seemed to be wearing a kind of coat made of yellow wool over a white shirt. And I don't think he's a knight. Nor a squire. Some kind of artist, I think.' She hesitated a moment, then plunged into a deeper confidence. 'And this is a secret. His name's Sam.'

'Sam?' cried Ninette and Alison together.

'Sam,' she repeated with obvious satisfaction. 'Isn't that sweet? And another thing I didn't tell you about him – he can blow smoke out of his mouth.'

'Like a dragon?' said Alison, astonished.

'No, not a bit like a dragon. Not blowing *angrily*, but *nicely*.'

'Perhaps he's an enchanter,' said Ninette.

This annoyed the Princess. 'No, he isn't. Just because your aunt was supposed to be a sorceress, Ninette, you've got sorcerers, wizards and enchanters on the brain – '

There was a tremendous knocking on the door, which was flung open to admit King Meliot's herald, a boozy fat man who had an enormous voice. 'Noble Princess Melicent – ladies,' he began, 'I beg to announce His Royal Majesty, King Meliot of Peradore – High Lord of Bergamore, Marralore and Parlot – Overlord of Lancington, Low Moss and Three Bridges!'

'I think you overdo those places,' said Melicent crossly. 'Who cares about Low Moss and Three Bridges?'

Before the herald could reply, there was a loud flourish

of trumpets just outside the door. The girls covered their
ears and pulled disgusted faces. Then King Meliot made his
entrance, not impressively because he was in too much of a
hurry. He was wearing his lightest crown and robes that had
once been gorgeous but were now shabby and not entirely
free from egg- and wine-stains. He was one of those worried-
looking middle-aged men in authority who imagine they are
being efficient when in fact they are only being over-busy in
a muddled fashion. He talked in a quick staccato manner, so
eager to have his say that he often interrupted himself.

'Morning, Melicent! Morning, girls!' he said as they curtsied. 'Not started work yet? Tapestry production has gone
down seventy-five per cent since we lost our dear Queen. It
won't do. Look to it. Well now, we've just received a summons to attend a conference at Camelot.'

The girls brightened up at once. 'When do we go?' said
Melicent.

'You don't. Men only – not even queens invited. Defence
problems. In any case Camelot these days isn't the place for
young unmarried daughters. Queen Guenevere – charming
woman of course – but – well – '

'Don't be absurd, Father,' said Melicent. 'We all know
about her and Sir Lancelot – '

'You don't,' the King shouted, suddenly angry. 'Nobody
does. All dam' nonsense!'

'Well then, if it's nonsense,' said Melicent, 'why can't – '

But her father refused to hear any more. 'Don't try to
argue, girl. You've no reason, no logic. Quiet now. We want
to think. Why are we here? Oh – yes, we want to take our
dwarf, Grumet, to Camelot. What have you done with him?'

'Oh – Father darling, you can't take Grumet to Camelot
again,' Melicent protested. 'He can't talk – and he's only got
three boring tricks.'

'Quite enough. And the one with the venison pasty was a
remarkable success last time. Sir Pelleas offered us a master

armourer for him. No, must have Grumet. Where is he? Speak up, child, speak up.'

Melicent was very hesitant. 'Well, Father – the fact is – I've sent him to find somebody – '

'Find somebody?' the King shouted. 'Who? Where? Why?'

'Well – you remember Master Malgrim, the enchanter – ?'

'Yes. New fella. Came with a letter from King Mark, wanting our patronage. Didn't take to him much. Too big for his boots. What about him?'

'He lent me a magic mirror,' said Melicent, still hesitant. 'It shows you anybody who's thinking about you – '

'Nonsense! You girls will believe anything. Where is it?'

Melicent handed him the mirror, and he stared at it for a moment or two. 'Just as we thought. Our own face, that's all.'

'You have to stare hard, sire,' said Ninette, who felt she had been silent long enough.

'We *are* staring hard,' said the King, still looking. 'Oh – but who's this? Looks like Sir Kay, who runs the palace at Camelot. Yes – and he's thinking about us.'

'All of us?' said Melicent.

'No, no – kingly us – *me*. And – by George – he's deciding to put us into the same cold draughty apartment on the north side we had before. But this time we won't have it. Here – take the thing. And what's it got to do with our dwarf? Didn't you say you'd sent him to find somebody?' He regarded his daughter with some suspicion.

'Yesterday,' Melicent began dreamily, 'I looked into the mirror, and I saw a man called Sam who was thinking about me. He was sweet.'

'Sweet? Nonsense! And who is this Sam? Never heard of him. And do you mean to say you sent our dwarf with a message to this rascal?'

'I asked Master Malgrim, the enchanter,' said Melicent, 'to lend his magic aid so that Grumet the dwarf could find Sam.

Because Sam's not in this realm, nor in any other known to
us – '

'Where is he then?'

'Well, Sam's not in what you'd call *real life* at all – '

'Oh – why didn't you say so?' King Meliot was delighted.
'Been stuffing yourself with mythology, legends, fairy tales

– eh? Very suitable, so long as you don't overdo it, my dear.
Well – well – send the dwarf along.'

'But I can't, Father. I told you, he's gone to find Sam.'

'What's the point,' the King demanded angrily, 'of sending
a real dwarf to find somebody who isn't real?'

'I didn't say Sam wasn't real – of course he is.'

'If he isn't in real life, then he isn't real.' The King was bellowing and glaring at her now. 'He's imaginary. Very well then – send an imaginary dwarf to find him. But what the devil's the point of sending a real dwarf? No logic, no reason, no sense! You must be suffering from summer green-sickness, girl.' He went to the door, and before he reached it he began shouting, 'Master Jarvie! Master Jarvie!'

After a few moments the long solemn face of the royal physician appeared round the door. He bowed, then looked enquiringly at the King.

'Princess Melicent – not us,' said the King impatiently. 'Suffering from delusions. Some kind of damsel nonsense. Says she sent Grumet the dwarf to find some fella who doesn't exist in real life. Obviously got a touch of something – '

'Father, I'm perfectly well – '

'Nonsense!'

'Your Highness,' said Jarvie as he approached her, 'allow me to observe that that is a statement few persons can make with any confidence to a physician of experience. You may *feel* perfectly well. But to *be* perfectly well – that is something very different. Permit me, Your Highness.'

'Keep still, child,' said the King. 'For your own good.'

The physician took her pulse, felt her forehead, pulled an eyelid down, looked at her tongue and made her say *Ah*. He himself kept saying *Um – um*.

'Well, what d'you make of it, Jarvie?' said the King impatiently. 'Tell us, man. Can't stay here all day.'

'The normal excellent balance of the four primary humours is somewhat disturbed,' said Jarvie, with immense gravity. 'The hot humours are not being sufficiently preserved in the blood by the thick, black and sour humours purged from the spleen. Or, as Galen tells us, the vital spirits formed in the heart are not being adequately checked by the natural spirits formed in the liver. Therefore, too quick release of the animal spirits formed in the brain – thus encouraging airy notions and fantasy – '

'There you have it,' cried the King. 'Airy notions and fantasy. The very thing that's wrong with the girl. What we'd do without science I can't imagine. What physic do you recommend, Jarvie?'

'A pearl dissolved in vinegar with powdered dragon's tooth, to be taken night and morning. Mummy paste and mandrake root in hot wine as a noon and evening posset. No venison nor pig puddings to be eaten. No scarlet to be worn. A bat's wing and a dried toad fastened beneath her shift until the new moon. And perhaps the thumb of a hanged man – '

'Never – never – never!' Melicent shook her head and stamped her foot.

The physician gave her a small condescending smile. 'Well, we may omit the thumb. But take the physic – '

'We'll see that she does,' said the King. 'You may go, Master Jarvie, and take our thanks with you.' He waved a hand, then turned to his daughter. 'Melicent, you stay close here.'

'Oh – Father – must I?'

'Certainly you must. Lady Ninette – Mistress Alison – see to it or we shall be severe with you. No gadding about. No damsel nonsense. Grumet the dwarf, I'll be bound, is lying drunk somewhere in this castle. If he should return here, send him to us at once.'

Melicent was in despair. 'But Master Malgrim swore he could send Grumet out of real life to where Sam is – '

King Meliot, who had moved towards the door, turned round to wag a finger at her. 'Malgrim's a charlatan. Grumet's a dumb little tosspot. You're a sick brain-fevered daydreaming damsel. Your Sam's a myth, a legend, a fairy-tale character, a romantic nothing. Now you know our commands, all of you – so obey 'em. Get out your needles and your threads. *We're* busy. *You* should be busy – busy, busy, busy, busy.' He opened the door, and shouted, 'No trumpets, no trumpets! Made enough noise this morning.' And off he went.

The three girls looked at one another in dismay. 'Tapestry now,' said Alison sadly.

'We ought to *make* something happen,' said Ninette. But for once she spoke without conviction, fire and wickedness.

Turning her back on them, Melicent said nothing. She stared at the blue and gold morning that had promised so much and had brought nothing but threats of mummy paste and mandrake root and all the other muck.

'What's the matter, Melicent darling?' said Alison.

Melicent's reply was muffled and faltering. 'I'm falling in love with Sam. And I don't know where he is – who he is – when he is – and now I don't believe Grumet can ever find him.' She burst into tears and hurried away.

Ninette and Alison looked at each other, murmuring, 'Poor Melicent!' their eyes sparkling with pleasure. Down the winding stair came the sound of a heavy door being slammed.

CHAPTER TWO

Sam and the Dwarf

Dan Dimmock ('Call me D.D., old man') of Wallaby, Dimmock, Paly and Tooks, the advertising agents, had a splendid room, the best in the place, with tall windows on two walls. Unfortunately, progress being rapid in that neighbourhood, there was coming through both sets of windows the sound of pneumatic drills. Dimmock was behind his big desk, staring at a sample lay-out. He was a fattish, worried, untidy man, always looking as if he had slept in the expensive clothes he wore, and he talked in a curious mixture of Lancashire and America, as if part of Madison Avenue had found its way into Burnley.

Facing him across the desk were two of his assistants, Anne Dutton-Swift and Philip Spencer-Smith. They were both in their early thirties and looked so much alike that they might have been twins, though in fact they were not related. But they were both tall and thin and quivering, U types forced into the rat-race.

'It doesn't do anything to me,' said Dimmock, throwing down the sample lay-out. 'It won't do anything to the client. And it's dead wrong for the Crunchy Choc public. Out!'

The pneumatic drills took over for the next forty-five seconds.

'Couldn't agree with you more, D.D.,' said Philip Spencer-Smith, when at last he could make himself heard.

'Publicwise it never looked good to me,' said Anne Dutton-Swift. 'But clientwise I'm not sure, D.D.'

'Well I am,' said Dimmock. 'It's out. Dead wrong for Crunchy Choc. What's next?'

'Damosel Stockings,' said Anne. 'I'm madly keen about this. Could be a big account. They want to spread themselves in the glossies visualwise. Romantic atmosphere. Sam Penty's working on it.'

Dimmock spoke into his intercom box. 'Peggy, ask Mr Penty to bring in what he's done for Damosel Stockings – sharp!'

'What I feel, D.D.,' said Anne, but the pneumatic drills began again. Dimmock swallowed two pills. Apparently Anne went on talking, for when the drills stopped, she said, 'Don't you agree?'

'Can't say,' Dimmock grunted. 'Never heard what you said with those dam' things going again.' He glared at the intercom box. 'Peggy, send another letter of complaint about these drills.' He took another pill and washed it down with a glass of water.

Sam Penty arrived, carrying a portfolio and smoking a bent cherrywood pipe. He was a square-faced chunky man in his thirties, and he wore a yellow pullover and paint-spattered corduroy trousers. 'Morning, D.D. Morning, Anne, Phil. Nice day.'

'Haven't noticed yet, Sam,' said Dimmock. 'Too much on my mind.'

'What's chiefly on my mind,' said Sam, 'is that today is the thirty-first of June.'

Dimmock stared at him. 'Thirty-first of June?'

Miss Dutton-Swift managed a silvery laugh. 'Don't be an idiot, Sammy. There isn't such a thing.'

Sam was unruffled. 'So everybody's been telling me. But I woke up feeling it was the thirty-first of June, and I can't get it out of my head.'

'Sam, I'll tell you something,' said Dimmock, still staring at him. 'I oughtn't to like you, but I do.'

'Same here, D.D.,' said Philip Spencer-Smith.

'Why do you keep on working for us?' Dimmock continued. 'I've often wondered.'

Sam looked thoughtful. 'Because I'm a bad painter. Not your idea of a bad painter, but my idea of one. So I work for Wallaby, Dimmock, Paly and Tooks – and eat. By the way, who the hell's Tooks? Or did you, Wallaby and Paly invent him?'

'Tooks is our financial man,' said Dimmock.

'First-class fellow,' said Philip.

'Smart as paint,' said Anne.

'That's right,' said Dimmock. 'And – between these four walls – a stinker. No, I oughtn't to have said that.'

'Why not?' Sam was now opening his portfolio. 'It's the thirty-first. Well, here we are.' He took out a brilliantly-coloured sketch of a girl and put it on a chair. It was in fact an excellent likeness of Princess Melicent of Peradore. 'This is what I've done for Damosel Stockings, and I sat up till two this morning getting it right. Now just take it in before you start talking.' But while Dimmock and Anne were taking it in, Sam pulled Phil away, to speak to him confidentially. 'Phil, who's this dwarf in red-and-yellow doublet and hose who's wandering about here this morning?'

'Dwarf? I haven't seen a dwarf.'

'He's around. Can't miss him if you see him at all.'

'Somebody in the art department must be using him as a model, Sam.'

'He never speaks. Just looks in at the door – grins – beckons – then vanishes.'

'Sam, old man, you're seeing things.'

'I hope so. It's my trade. But why a dwarf in red-and-yellow tights?'

Dimmock was now pronouncing judgment. 'It's got something.'

'Just what I was thinking, D.D.,' said Anne.

'On the other hand,' Dimmock added dubiously, 'I don't know –'

'Quite. The Damosel crowd are tough.'

'What do you think, Phil?'

'Feel what you do, D.D. Yes and no.'

'Let's stop looking for a minute,' said Dimmock, 'then take it by surprise.'

'Who was your model, Sam?' Anne asked him.

'Didn't have one. Not in this world anyhow. It's quite a story, but I don't have to tell it.'

'Why not?' said Dimmock. 'Let's have a drink. The usual? Peggy, we'll have four large gins and tonics.' No sooner had he given this order than a loud singing commercial came blasting through one wall, only to be defeated by the pneumatic drills shaking the windows. When there was something like quiet again, Dimmock continued gloomily: 'Nobody can say I'm not keen and sharp. I worry over the firm and the accounts sixteen hours a day – at least. But now and again I wonder if we aren't all barmy. Thanks, Peggy, hand 'em round.'

Peggy, his secretary, was a pretty mousy girl, and so exactly like Mistress Alison of Peradore that only a scientist would call it a coincidence.

'Thanks, Peggy,' said Sam as he took his drink. 'Have any of you girls seen a red-and-yellow dwarf?'

'No,' said Peggy, without a smile. 'Why, Mr Penty? Have you lost one?'

'No, but I keep seeing one.'

'Seeing one *what*, Sam?' Dimmock asked as Peggy went out. He laughed. 'For a moment I really thought you said a red-and-yellow dwarf.'

'That's what I did say,' said Sam. 'Well, here's to Wallaby, Dimmock, Paly – and possibly Tooks. Yesterday, when you gave me this Damosel job, I sat at my work table, thinking it over. Damosel – knights in armour – castles – King Arthur and the Round Table – dragons – quests – princesses in towers – you know, the old baloney. And then I saw a girl in medieval costume, through a kind of illuminated little frame, and she smiled at me. She stayed long enough for me to do a rough sketch. Then, twice later, when I was painting and wasn't sure about her colouring, she appeared again, very sensibly and charmingly, just when I needed her most.'

'I can see you're devoted to this girl, Sam,' said Anne.

'Certainly. Above all others. This is the girl for me.'

'And all imagination!' said Dimmock wonderingly.

'I dare say,' said Sam, 'but what's imagination? Nobody tells us – at least nobody who *has* any imagination. Well then, after sitting up half the night trying to recapture the look of her, I woke up this morning feeling it was the thirty-first of June – '

Dimmock cut in sharply. 'Sam, you know I'm your friend as well as one of your employers. Now will you do a little thing for me, as a favour?'

'Certainly, D.D.'

'Good enough.' Dimmock spoke into his box. 'Peggy, is Dr Jarvis still with Mr Paly? He is? Then ask him to come and see me.' He looked at Anne and Phil. 'You two had better go before Jarvis comes. This is between Sam and me and him. But look, Anne – before you go – I've got some sample Damosel stockings somewhere – ' he began rummaging round in his desk and then brought out several fine pairs of nylons – 'so just drape these round Sam's picture, so we make sure it all hangs together and one thing isn't cancelling out another and so forth – '

'Damosel will buy this,' said Anne, as she framed the picture in stockings. 'But I'll have to talk to them hard. Especially Maggie Rogers – she's got a *Vogue* fixation. There! Come on, Phil.'

'Anne ducky,' said Phil as they moved to the door, 'I'm not mad about our Mum's Chum lay-out. Minnie and Jeff have fallen down on it – '

Left to themselves, Sam and Dimmock looked at each other.

'But why a doctor?' said Sam.

'No harm in a quick check-up,' said Dimmock. 'And he's a first-class man. Among other things, consultant to the Healthovite company. This should be him. Come in.'

Dr Jarvis was exactly like Master Jarvie of Peradore. The only difference was that instead of wearing a long black gown, he now wore a short black coat and striped trousers.

'Hello, Dr Jarvis,' said Dimmock. 'This is Sam Penty, one of our best artists. And he's not getting his proper sleep. He's seeing things – girls and dwarfs. And he thinks today's the thirty-first of June.'

'So what?' Sam growled. 'I'm perfectly well.'

'Mr Penty,' said the doctor, going nearer to him, 'in my experience, very few people *are* perfectly well, although they may imagine they are. And you're probably an imaginative type – '

'He is, he is, Doctor,' said Dimmock.

'Now, Mr Penty, just relax. Allow me.' He took Sam's pulse, felt his forehead, pulled an eyelid down, looked at his tongue and made him say *Ah*. He himself kept saying *Um – um*.

'An eidetic type,' said Dr Jarvis, 'probably hyperthyroid – with an unstable metabolism involving both iodine and calcium deficits. May have been some recent effect of the adrenal cortex on the calcium metabolism antagonistic to the functioning of the parathyroid glands. Some possible kidney trouble – insomnia – over-stimulation of the eidetic image-creating function, chiefly due to parathyroid deficiency and a heightening of the thyroid function, so a definite thyroid-parathyroid imbalance, resulting in an apparent objectiviza-tion of the imagery of the eidetic imagination – fantasy states – hallucinations – '

'That's it, Doctor,' cried Dimmock triumphantly. 'Fantasy states and hallucinations. Just what Sam's suffering from. Now can't you give him something that'll put him right?'

'I'll tell my chemist to send round some calcium and vitamin D tablets, to be taken three times a day. I'll have him make up a mixture with hexamine, quinic acid and theobromine in it – to be taken twice a day. A bromide mixture too, night and morning. Avoid an excess of alcohol and too many carbohydrates.'

'There you are, Sam. First-class, Doctor. You went straight to the root of the trouble. Very grateful.'

'Glad to be of service,' said Dr Jarvis. 'Good morning, gentlemen.' And out he went, to be of service elsewhere.

'He'll put it right,' said Dimmock. 'I'll bet in a day or two, Sam, you're not seeing things.'

'I like seeing things.'

'But you know what can happen to people who see things other people don't see?'

'Yes,' said Sam, 'they're in the National Gallery.'

Dimmock began looking through the papers on his desk. 'No, I mean chaps who think it's the thirty-first of June – you had me guessing there for a minute, Sam – and chaps who begin asking about red-and-yellow dwarfs in tights.' He did not look up as he went on talking. If he had done he would have seen that Grumet the dwarf, dressed in red-and-yellow doublet and hose, had now arrived in the room, not by way of the door but apparently out of the cupboard. 'Even while your own common sense tells you we don't have red-and-yellow dwarfs here – wouldn't know what to do with one if we had one – and that it stands to reason it's nothing but your own imagination – '

Sam checked him. 'Pst!' He indicated the dwarf, who was now capering, grinning, and pointing at Sam.

'Hells bells!' Dimmock roared. 'Here – you!'

With a last mischievous flourish at Sam, the dwarf grabbed the picture and the stockings, ran with them and dived clean through the cupboard.

'He's taken my picture,' said Sam angrily. 'Hoy – hoy!'

'Stop him,' cried Dimmock, coming round the desk. 'Stop him.'

Together they flung open the cupboard doors, only to find it solidly filled with books and files, without any trace of the dwarf. Dimmock looked at Sam in dismay. 'He couldn't have gone through there.'

'He could. He did. And I think he came in through this cupboard.'

'Stop it, Sam,' said Dimmock irritably. 'You've got me going now.' He began ringing bells on his desk. They brought Anne and Phil back into the room, looking anxious.

'I'm now quitting these premises,' Sam announced firmly. 'And I don't propose to return today, which I'm still convinced is the thirty-first.'

'What – you're going home, Sam?' said Dimmock.

'I'm going to my local – the Black Horse in Peacock Place – which should be open by the time I get there. And if I were you three, I'd pack up all pretence of work. *It's the wrong day.*' And Sam hurried out.

'D.D.,' Anne began reproachfully, 'you oughtn't to have let him go before we decided about the Damosel thing. Where's his picture?' She looked round urgently. 'Look, D.D., he must have taken it.'

'No, he didn't.'

'But, D.D., it's not here. *Somebody* must have taken it.'

Phil gave her a thin sketch of a grin. 'Perhaps a red-and-yellow dwarf, ducky.'

Dimmock ignored them. 'Peggy, bring me two aspirins and a glass of water.'

'Stop clowning, Phil,' said Anne severely. 'This is business now. D.D. – *did* somebody take it?'

'Yes.' Dimmock spoke heavily and very slowly, breathing hard. 'A red-and-yellow dwarf. He dived into that cupboard with it – '

Anne smiled, but reproachfully. 'Now, D.D., please – '

The eruption came. 'I tell you,' Dimmock shouted at the top of his voice, *'a red-and-yellow dwarf ran away with it.* He dived – oh damn and blast!' For now the pneumatic drills were back again, and, no longer able to make himself heard, Dimmock in his rage flung papers in the air and began drumming on his desk.

CHAPTER THREE

The Two Enchanters

In the tapestry chamber in King Meliot's castle, Melicent and Ninette were pretending to listen to Lamison playing his lute. (Where was Alison? Was she, as Peggy the secretary, now bringing Dimmock his two aspirins and a glass of water?) Lamison finished his performance with a flourish and several wrong notes, and then got up and bowed.

'Thank you, Lamison,' said Melicent graciously. 'Very nice – but we're just not in the mood. So you may go.'

Ninette gave him a hard look. 'And try to learn "The Black Knight Hath My Heart".'

Melicent was peevish as soon as Lamison had gone. 'Who wants a black knight anyhow? Or any colour, for that matter? I think knights are so *boring*.'

'I've said so a million times, darling.'

'All that idiotic clattering and clashing and banging! All that buckling and unbuckling! I ask you.'

'You needn't,' said Ninette. 'I ruined my nails helping to unbuckle Sir Maris, that day at the Astolat Tournament. And then he talked about nothing but heraldry for hours and hours until I could have screamed, my dear. What I'd like is an enchanter.'

'It's what we'd all like, Ninette dear.'

'No, I mean a professional, a properly qualified magician.'

Melicent pulled a face. 'They're always so *old*.'

'Yes, but a really clever one, if you insisted, could make himself seem any age you fancied.'

'I know. But I'd still feel really he was old, and a bit smelly –'

'All you're thinking about is your Sam.'

'I keep telling myself not to,' said Melicent sadly. 'Yesterday was wonderful. But today – what is there?'

'We ought to *make* things happen,' Ninette told her.

'With my assistance, I hope, ladies. At your service, most noble Princess.' The speaker was standing before them, apparently having arrived from nowhere. He was tall and handsome in a rather sinister style, with a long sharp nose and a blue-black moustache and short beard. He was magnificently gowned in the sorcerer fashion, with various signs of the zodiac embroidered in gold and silver thread. He had one of those very careful voices that always sound slightly foreign in all languages.

'Master Malgrim,' said Melicent in her best regal manner, 'you're not supposed to make sudden appearances like this. It's not allowed. Ninette – this is Master Malgrim, the new enchanter who came from King Mark. Lady Ninette.'

He bowed, and Ninette smiled at him. 'Master Malgrim, how did you do it?'

'I was invisible of course,' he replied, in a tone of affable condescension. 'A quick simple method most of us use now. Only very old-fashioned magicians and enchanters, these days, still prefer to transform themselves. For example, my uncle, who insisted upon coming along, decided to enter the castle and make his way up here – as a brown rat. Not here yet, I suppose? No? That proves my point – a risky, clumsy, slow method.'

'I hope he's not coming in here as a brown rat,' said Melicent.

'He's apt to be mischievous,' said Malgrim, 'and too fond of showing off. His name's Marlagram, by the way. One of the old Merlin school.'

Ninette, who from the first had regarded him with open admiration, now exclaimed, 'I think you're marvellous, Master Malgrim.'

'Professionally I have to be marvellous, of course. But if

you meant it personally, Lady Ninette, then I'm flattered and delighted.' He smiled and bowed. 'But now, Princess Melicent, I must ask for the return of my mirror. You have it here, I think? Ah yes – allow me. Please don't look so disappointed. Its power soon begins to fail if one person uses it frequently. You must have noticed that.'

Melicent cheered up at once. 'Then perhaps Sam *has* been thinking about me today. And the wretched mirror just wouldn't let me see him. But where's Grumet the dwarf? And did he find Sam? Tell me – quick – Master Malgrim.'

He shrugged his shoulders and spread out his fingers, all in a very un-English manner, and said rather loftily, 'You go too fast, noble Princess. Remember – I was refused an appointment as Court Magician and Official Enchanter to the Kingdom of Peradore. Meanwhile, thanks to my powerful and extremely skilful aid, Grumet the dwarf has now returned, carrying strange beautiful gifts.'

'From Sam? Oh – heavenly! Where *is* Grumet?' Melicent almost danced in her impatience.

'Ah – where indeed? No doubt one of your official Court Enchanters could inform you.'

'You know very well we haven't any now.'

'Melicent, dear,' said Ninette, 'you just can't afford to be high-and-mighty with him. He's *much* too clever.' She smiled invitingly at Malgrim, who bowed his acknowledgment.

'What do I have to do then, Master Malgrim?' said Melicent.

Obviously a plotty type, Malgrim did not hesitate for a second. 'Years ago, when your father was a young knight, Merlin gave him a gold brooch. Now – to be perfectly frank – if I could steal it, I would. But no gift of Merlin's can be stolen. You or your father, of your own free will, must hand it over to me. Give me your promise that this shall be done, and I will help you to your heart's desire. But first, before you can even see the dwarf and the gifts he brings, I must have your solemn promise.'

While Melicent was still hesitating, a voice cried, 'Don't do it. Don't do it. No solemn promises.' A little old man was there, cackling and muttering and darting about. The girls screamed, and Malgrim looked furious. This could only be his uncle, Marlagram. He had a long beard and was shabbily dressed, with nothing magnificent about him, and he seemed to be an ancient rustic kind of enchanter, well in with trolls, gnomes and elves. But in spite of his aged appearance, he was a very lively old magician indeed, seemingly filled with a diabolical sort of energy. His favourite noise was a very high chuckle-cackle, most inadequately represented by *he-he-he!*

'My uncle,' said Malgrim with chilly disgust, 'Master Marlagram.'

'Don't trouble to tell me who they are, Nephew. I know, I know, I know – *he-he-he!*' He pointed a long and very dirty finger. 'You're Princess Melicent – an' a nice ripe, tasty piece o' damselry too – an' if I were only ninety again you'd get no Sam through me – I'd attend to you meself – *he-he-he!*'

'I think you're a disgusting old man,' said Melicent, but not too unpleasantly.

'You're quite right, girl, I am,' said Marlagram cheerfully. 'But I'm also very very very very clever, as you'll soon find out. *He-he-he!*' Now he pointed at Ninette and went closer to her. 'Here's a wicked wench – oh, a mischievous piece o' saucy goods you are – an' what a hanky-panky, hocus-pocus, lawdy-bawdy future you have, girl!'

'I can take it,' said Ninette coolly.

The indefatigable ancient started capering about. 'An' it's all on its way – lawdy-bawdy, hocus-pocus, hanky-panky – *he-he-he!*'

'Showing off,' said Malgrim coldly. 'It never stops. So tasteless and tedious. Brings discredit to our whole profession.' He wagged a finger at his uncle. 'I told you I'd be here first. Beat you by about ten minutes.'

'Ger-out-cher! I'd a bit o' roguish business to attend to down below.' He looked at Melicent now, his eyes below the shaggy brows glittering like glass in a dusty hedge. 'See what he's up to, my dear? Trying to make you believe his old uncle's out-of-date. But I know a lot o' tricks he's never learnt yet. I was serving my time with Merlin before this fellow-me-lad was born – *he-he-he!* You're waiting for Grumet the dwarf, aren't you?'

'Yes,' said Melicent eagerly. 'Where is he?'

'He'll be here,' said Malgrim hastily, 'as soon as I have your promise – '

But his uncle cut him short. 'Don't believe him, don't believe him, my dear. He can't produce the dwarf – *he-he-he!* I've seen to that.'

'Uncle, this is intolerable,' said Malgrim angrily. 'I warned you not to interfere – '

'*He-he-he!*'

'Do you ask for a trial of strength, you foolish old man?'

'I do, I do, I do. *He-he-he!* A sporting contest – one round only – Merlin rules – winner takes the Princess to Sam.'

'So be it,' said Malgrim grandly, drawing himself up. 'Now – *I command you.*'

The girls cried out in alarm and shrank from the two magicians, who were glaring at each other through a sinister twilight that had suddenly invaded the room.

'Go on, boy,' cried old Marlagram, still capering away. 'Command your head off. *He-he-he!*'

Malgrim looked terrible, and spoke terribly in some magic language that sounded like *Vartha gracka – Marlagram – oh terrarma vava marvagrista demogorgon!* In what was almost darkness now, there was a growl of thunder, a flash of lightning, and a horrid smell of sulphur. The girls, clutching each other, pressed themselves against the wall.

But if Malgrim had been impressive, his old uncle was now even more so, in the same style. '*Vartha gracka – Malgrim,*' he screamed. '*Oh terra marveena groodumagisterra Beelzebub!*' This was followed by a terrific crack of thunder and a flash of lightning that blinded the two girls. When at last they came out of their terrified huddle and opened their eyes, they saw that the darkness had vanished, and with it all trace of Malgrim. There was old Marlagram alone, grinning and chuckling.

'All over,' he told them. 'No need to be frightened, my dears. He's gone – and serve him right. Too conceited by half – an' no proper respect for his elders.'

'But what's happened?' Melicent still felt dazed. 'I don't understand, Master Marlagram.'

'Very simple, my dear. *He-he-he!* I'm looking after you now. And I make no conditions, don't ask for any solemn promises – notice that. You trust me, I'll trust you. The good old-fashioned style. Now if it's this Sam you want, then I'll take you to him wherever he is. *He-he-he!* But first you want to see the dwarf, don't you? Grumet,' he called, 'Grumet, Grumet. Come, boy, come, boy, come, boy.'

There was a sudden brightness in the chamber, and with it came the whistling sound of wind, and then Grumet was there, carrying the portrait and the stockings, grinning and capering.

'Oh Grumet, did you see him?' said Melicent. 'And what have you brought? Is this the picture of me that Sam painted? Oh look – look, Ninette – isn't it wonderful?'

Ninette looked. 'The nose isn't right.'

'Of course it is,' said Melicent indignantly. 'You're only jealous. The nose is *perfect*. It's a marvellous portrait of me. How clever of Sam! Now what are these? Stockings? Oh – look at them – look – look – '

This time Ninette was equally excited. 'They're so – so – *sheer*. It must be an enchantment.'

'I must try them on.'

'What about me?'

'No, Ninette, not while you're feeling so jealous – '

'Stop,' said Marlagram. 'You wish to see this Sam?'

'Of course. You said you'd take me to him.'

'Then get ready. We start in an hour,' said Marlagram. 'No sooner, no later. I've an hour's work to do before we can find this Sam. He isn't round the corner, y'know – at least not what *you'd* call round the corner. In space maybe, but not in time. So I need an hour to work it out. Then we'll go – *he-he-he!* Grumet, stay here, boy. Now I'm off.' He vanished in the brightness and the whistling wind.

'I'm sorry, Ninette,' said Melicent, preparing to take her treasures away, 'but you'll have to stay here. You've never been really sympathetic about Sam, so I feel I ought to leave you out of this.' Then she hurried out.

Ninette looked with disgust at Grumet, who was now squatting against a pillar. 'If you could only talk, you stupid little thing. Is it really hard to find this Sam person?' The dwarf nodded an emphatic yes. 'Can't be done without magic, I suppose?' The dwarf shook an equally emphatic no.

'Not that I want him, of course. I think the whole thing's ridiculous. But I refuse to be treated like this without doing *something*. I'm not going to be left out of everything as if I didn't count at all. If only Master Malgrim hadn't been so easily defeated – '

'No, Lady Ninette,' said Malgrim, apparently stepping out of the pillar, 'I must correct you there. Actually it was a very near thing. The truth is, my uncle – who, after all, is a cunning old hand – had prepared himself for that contest and I hadn't. Now – it's my move.'

'Can't I do something?'

'You can.' Malgrim came closer and lowered his voice, very much the plotter now. 'As soon as the Princess leaves with my uncle, be prepared to receive Sam.'

'Sam? But they're going to find him.'

'Yes, but they won't find him. And why? Because I shall find him first. *Ha-ha!* I'll bring him back here while they're still looking for him there. When he arrives, you will entertain him. So be prepared.'

'Master Malgrim,' said Ninette with enthusiasm, 'I adore you.'

'You flatter me, Lady Ninette,' said Malgrim in his best high society manner. 'And now, if you'll excuse me, I must read this manikin's mind. Come here, Grumet.' He stared hard at the dwarf, as if he were reading a badly-printed page. Then he looked at Ninette. 'Remember what you must do, Lady Ninette.'

'Of course. Leave Sam to me.'

'We go then.' He put a hand on the dwarf's shoulder. The wind from nowhere whistled through the sudden brightness. Magician and dwarf vanished.

Before deciding what she should wear for Sam, Ninette allowed herself a few moments of self-congratulation. She was in the mood to coin a phrase. 'The plot,' she told herself delightedly, 'thickens.'

CHAPTER FOUR

In the Black Horse

The Black Horse in Peacock Place is a little oasis in the desert of brick and stucco that lies between South Kensington Underground Station and the Fulham Road. Its small Private Bar, on this particular morning, was so select and quiet that it contained only one fat middle-aged customer and one thin middle-aged barmaid. Their talk, over the customer's pint of mild and bitter, was not unusual but was not a good example of the native wit, the folk philosophy, the keen criticism of life, for which the English pub is famous.

'No,' the thin barmaid was saying, with a complete absence of interest, 'he come in 'ere Tuesday, Mr Sanderson did.'

The fat man thought this over. 'Ar. He told me Wednesday.'

'Might 'ave bin Wednesday,' the barmaid slowly conceded. 'But I'd 'ave said Tuesday.'

The fat man was also a fair man. 'He could 'ave made a mistake when he said it was Wednesday.'

'That's right,' said the barmaid. There was a long pause. A clock ticked somewhere. A ray of sunlight got itself entangled among the bottles of liqueurs behind and above the barmaid's head. 'But I might be wrong when I say it was Tuesday, mightn't I?'

'That's right,' said the fat man. He listened to the buzzing of a bluebottle, as if it might have some opinion of its own about Mr Sanderson's movements. 'Anyhow, must 'ave bin either Tuesday *or* Wednesday.'

'That's right,' said the barmaid.

Sam Penty came bursting in. 'Good morning! Good morning!'

'Mornin',' said the barmaid lifelessly. 'Turned out nice again.'

'It has, it has. Double gin and a glass of mild, please.' As she turned to serve him, Sam looked at the fat man, who was staring into his pint as if he might find Mr Sanderson there. 'In fact, I don't remember a nicer thirty-first of June. Do you?'

'No, I don't,' said the fat man. But then, feeling uneasy, he took out a pocket-book and began frowning at it, finally looking suspiciously from it to Sam, who was now receiving and paying for his drinks.

'Thank you,' said Sam to the barmaid. 'And how are – er – things?'

'Quiet,' she told him. She looked at the fat man. 'But I'd say it was Tuesday Mr Sanderson come in 'ere.'

'I don't say it wasn't,' said the fat man with great earnestness. 'But Wednesday he said it was.'

'That's right.' Then, after some thought: 'But that could 'ave bin his mistake, couldn't it?'

'It could.' The fat man finished his mild and bitter. 'Then again, you could be wrong when you say it was Tuesday, couldn't you?'

'That's right. Could 'ave bin Wednesday like you say.'

'If it wasn't Tuesday,' said the fat man gloomily. 'Well, must be getting along. Oh reservoir!'

'Ta-ta for now!'

'Good-bye!' said Sam cheerfully as the fat man went out. Sam swallowed the gin and then tasted the beer.

'Bin quiet all the week,' said the barmaid very slowly and sadly.

'What about when Mr Sanderson was in here?'

'You mean Tuesday?'

'Yes, yes – '

'Or Wednesday,' the barmaid added thoughtfully.

'Yes, yes, yes.'

'Do you know Mr Sanderson?'

'No, I don't.'

'Neither do I except that he's a bookie,' said the barmaid
bitterly. 'Don't know what he looks like an' don't care neither.
But you 'ave to say something, 'aven't you?'

At that moment a man came rushing in as if the Private
Bar were a train he had to catch. ''Morning, 'morning!' he
shouted. 'Two double scotches, dear – like lightning.'

He was a rather large, plump man, wearing a loud suit
that was too tight for him. He had a bristling red face that
suggested an over-ripe gooseberry. As the barmaid began
measuring out his whiskies, he turned to Sam. 'What will
you have, sir?' He had the voice and manner of those men
who at all times of day and night are never quite drunk and
never quite sober.

Sam indicated his glass. 'Nothing just now, thanks. Got
one.'

'Please yourself, old boy. Ever done a deal in flat-bottomed
boats?'

Sam said he hadn't.

'Then don't. It's hell. I've been plastered since the end of
April – mostly in Cornwall. Hate the bloody place. You've
heard of me – Cap'n Plunket?'

'I don't think so,' said Sam.

'Course you have, old boy. Remember that film I intro-
duced – all about the fish that climbs a tree. Same man. Pat
Plunket – the Old Skipper. Turn up anywhere, everywhere.
"Here's good old Skip Plunket," they all say.' He threw a ten-
shilling note on the bar counter. 'Thank you, dear. Keep the
change.' He downed one of the doubles at a gulp.

Sam looked at him. 'Who *are* these people who all say
"Good old Skip Plunket"?'

He turned triumphantly to the barmaid. 'There you are,
dear. What did I say? He knew me all right. Everybody does.
What's the date?'

'Thirty-first of June,' Sam replied promptly.

'And about time too,' said Plunket. 'Ought to be in Genoa now. I've got eighty cases of damaged custard powder there. Bought 'em off a fella in Barcelona. He was plastered. So was I. What the hell can you do with damaged custard powder?'

'Turn it into damaged custard, I suppose,' said Sam thoughtfully. 'You'd need a good advertising campaign. *Are You Still Eating Undamaged Custard?* That sort of thing. Try Mr Dimmock of Wallaby, Dimmock, Paly and Tooks. Ignore Tooks.'

'Thanks for the tip, old boy. How'd you feel about a half share in a disused Portuguese lighthouse?'

'It would have to be the top half,' said Sam. 'And very cheap.'

'Drop me a line week after next. Care of the Albanian Sports Club, Old Compton Street. Know it, old boy?'

'No, old boy.'

'Filthy hole. What did you say your name was?'

'I didn't. But it's Penty – Sam Penty.'

'Of course. Knew your brother in Nairobi.'

'I haven't got a brother.'

'It was somebody else then,' said Plunket. 'But it just shows you what a damned small world we live in.' He swallowed his second double. 'Where's the phone, dear?'

'In the passage, back of the Saloon,' said the barmaid. 'You'll have to go out, then in again.'

'Anybody know the number of the Panamanian Legation? No? Never mind.' Plunket looked as if he were going out but then suddenly wheeled round, beckoning Sam to go nearer.

'What d'you think about this deal, old boy? I've a third share in an electric guitar band arriving from Venezuela next Thursday, if all goes well. Now a fella I met in Polperro night before last – he was a bit plastered – offered me in exchange for this third share a thirty per cent holding in a pilchard canning company. You're a keen fella — what do *you* feel?'

'I don't like tinned pilchards,' said Sam. 'But then I don't like electric guitars either. By the way, what would *you* feel if you kept seeing a dwarf in red-and-yellow doublet and hose?'

Plunket showed no surprise at being asked this question. 'Oh – he's looking for you, is he?'

Sam was staggered. 'Do you mean he's *here*?'

'Outside a minute ago, old boy. Well, shan't be long. Don't go.'

As soon as Plunket had gone, it was almost as if the place had closed. Sam looked at the barmaid, and she looked at nothing.

'Quiet, isn't it?' said Sam.

'That's right,' said the barmaid.

Staring about him idly, Sam looked towards the door just in time to see it open. Into the opening came the head and shoulders of the dwarf, who recognized him, grinned broadly, then vanished.

'Look here,' said Sam excitedly, 'did *you* see a dwarf in red-and-yellow?'

'When?' asked the barmaid.

'Just now. When the door opened.'

'Saw the door blow open, that's all,' said the barmaid.

'Okay, you win.' Sam sounded resigned. 'But I'll have another double gin and glass of mild, please.'

When she put the drinks on the counter, she said to him, 'You think I'm stupid, don't you?'

This took Sam by surprise. 'Well – not exactly – no. But – er – '

'Of course you do,' said the barmaid severely. 'Well, let me tell you something. If I didn't make myself stupid on this job, in a week I'd be round the flamin' bend. An' that'll be four an' ten.'

The man who came in now was a very impressive figure but looked out of place in his black-and-white magnificence. He might have been an old-fashioned conjurer on the grand

scale, about to begin his performance. When Sam stared at him, he smiled and said, 'Good morning, Sam!'

'Oh – hello!' Sam tried not to show his surprise. 'Let's see – did I meet you at one of Natasha's parties – theatrical types? Not an illusionist, are you?'

'How clever of you, Sam. That is exactly what I am. Malgrim is the name.' He turned to the barmaid and then pointed. 'I will have that bottle there – the green one.'

'The creem de menthy? But not the whole bottle?'

'If you please.' He pointed to a large silver tankard, kept as an ornament. 'I'll pour it into that. You want money, of course.' He produced a thick handful of notes and carelessly threw them on to the counter.

''Ere, steady on!' cried the barmaid, putting down the bottle of crème-de-menthe and the tankard.

'Don't keep them long, that's all,' said Malgrim, pouring the liqueur into the tankard. 'They'll be dead leaves soon. But they won't change while it's still the thirty-first.'

'The thirty-first, eh?' said Sam. 'Did you see a dwarf out there?'

'I did. Grumet's his name. He's in my employment for the time being.'

'He is, is he?' Sam was indignant. 'Well, he ran away with my painting.'

'Ah yes – the portrait of Princess Melicent. Well, she's seen it – she's delighted with it – and is longing to make your acquaintance, Sam. That's why I'm here.' He raised the tankard. 'Well, my respects and best wishes, Sam.'

'Stop 'im,' said the barmaid, now thoroughly alarmed. 'He'll be unconscious in a minute – a whole bottle of creem de menthy!'

'Very refreshing,' said Malgrim, after having drained the tankard. 'Now, Sam – I want to keep our talk free from any professional pedantry if I can, but how familiar are you with the problems of higher space?'

'I'm not,' said Sam. 'Who's Princess Melicent?'

'Suppose we assume a universe of six dimensions,' said Malgrim. 'The first three are length, breadth and thickness. The next three might be called – first, the sphere of attention and material action; second, the sphere of memory; third, the sphere of imagination. Are you following me?'

'No,' said Sam. 'What do you mean when you say you're here because this princess wants to make my acquaintance?'

'Whatever is imagined must exist somewhere in the universe.'

'That's right,' said the barmaid.

'Now, Sam, you probably think Princess Melicent is an imaginary figure.'

'Well, I do and I don't,' Sam said carefully.

'Quite right,' said Malgrim, smiling. 'Because of course she is and she isn't. And while she knows that she herself is in real life, she naturally feels you must be outside it, as of course I do –'

'Wait a minute.' Sam was rather indignant. 'Do you mean you don't call this real life?'

'Of course not. A horrible confused botch of dreams, nightmares, fantasies and mixed partial enchantments. But of course it exists – just as you exist in it – and you too, of course, my dear lady.'

'Much obliged,' said the barmaid. 'I was getting worried.'

'Where does my painting come in?' Sam asked suspiciously.

'It doesn't yet,' said Malgrim. 'I'm now explaining how it is possible – once you know the trick – to go from our world to yours, from yours to ours. I leave real life for imaginary life – and meet you. When you go back with me – as I trust you will, shortly – then you leave real life for imaginary life, to meet the Princess. Which is real, which is imaginary, depends upon the position of the observer. It could truthfully be said that both are real, both are imaginary.'

'What about that dwarf – which is he?'

'Not quite either at the moment. I've just sent him home.'

The door was flung open. It was the Old Skipper, Cap'n Plunket, again.

'Now 'e's back,' the barmaid muttered. 'That's all we needed.'

'Two double scotches, dear. What about you two?'

'No, thanks. Got one,' said Sam. 'Captain Plunket – Mr Malgrim, the illusionist.'

'Of course,' said Plunket, shaking hands enthusiastically. 'Couldn't place you for a moment. Seen you at the Savage Club. Remember you at the Holborn Empire too. Wonderful act. There's ten bob, dear. Keep the change. Happy days!'

'You sent the dwarf home?' Sam said to Malgrim. 'But where's that?'

'The kingdom of Peradore.'

'Can't say I know it,' said Plunket. 'But knew a fella called Peradore. He'd six fingers on each hand. Never kept his hands still, though. Chaps nearly went barmy trying to count his fingers.'

'Peradore?' Sam said slowly to Malgrim. 'It sounds to me like something out of the Arthurian legends. And if it is, how can anybody *go* there?'

'In the third sphere,' said Malgrim, smooth as butter, 'are parallel times, diverging and converging times, and times spirally intertwined.'

'It just shows you,' said Plunket. 'And, talking of times, I can put you on to a fella who has four gross of Swiss watches in the spare tank of his motor yacht. Daren't land 'em. He's hot as a stove.' He swallowed his second double. 'Let's have a spot of lunch. Troc or somewhere. On me.'

Malgrim looked grave and shook his head. 'Sam and I must go to Peradore.'

'Been closed for years, old boy, if it's the place I think you mean. Better try the Troc. And anyhow you wouldn't ditch good old Skip Plunket, would you?'

'Yes,' said Malgrim.

'Can't be done, old boy.' He put an arm across Sam's shoulders. 'Sam and I are up to our necks in a custard-powder deal and a Portuguese lighthouse. If you want to try the old Peradore, I'm game, though ten to one we'll end up at the Troc. But where Sam goes, I go.'

'Then take the consequences,' said Malgrim sharply.

'Old Skip Plunket is always ready – '

'*Silence!*' The wind that came whistling up from nowhere seemed to blow the wall away. It went roaring down a tunnel where the wall had been. And three big solid men just vanished. The last thing the barmaid remembered, before she went off into a faint, was hearing the conjurer chap saying, 'Gentlemen – welcome to Peradore!'

She had just given herself a drop of brandy when Anne Dutton-Swift and Philip Spencer-Smith arrived, tall and spruce, keen and brisk.

'Good morning!' said Anne brightly.

'Good morning!' said Philip, just as brightly.

The barmaid did her best. ' 'Mornin'. Turned,' she continued, slowly and faintly, 'out – nice – again.'

'It has, hasn't it?' said Philip. 'You're quiet in here, aren't you?'

'That's right.' The barmaid closed her eyes.

'We're really looking for a friend,' said Anne, wasting a charming smile on the barmaid's closed eyes.

'He said he was coming along here,' said Philip.

'Mr Sam Penty – '

'Have you seen him this morning?'

The barmaid opened her eyes. 'Yes. 'E's bin in.'

'Oh – jolly good!' said Philip, who felt the poor woman needed some encouragement.

'Now, can you tell us what's happened to him?' said Anne, who was as loud and clear as if she were addressing a mentally defective child or a foreigner.

'Come closer,' said the barmaid rather faintly. 'Just 'ad a nasty turn.'

'Oh – rotten luck!' said Philip.

'Don't force yourself,' said Anne as she moved closer.

'I'll 'ave to,' said the barmaid, obviously making an effort. 'Now you can believe me or believe me not – '

'But of course – we believe you – '

' 'Im an' two other crackpots went off together. Something about a princess – an' a Portuguese light'ouse – six fingers an' Swiss watches – '

'Sorry,' said Philip, 'but you're not making this awfully clear – '

'But don't worry,' said Anne. 'Just tell us *where* they went.'

The barmaid pointed a shaking finger. 'As true as I'm 'ere. Through that wall. They went through it an' left me 'alf up it.'

Anne and Philip looked at the wall, looked at the barmaid, looked at each other. 'Back to the office, Phil,' said Anne. 'And I don't think D.D. is going to like this.'

CHAPTER FIVE

End of Mr Dimmock's Morning

Mr Dimmock in fact was not liking anything. About the time when Anne Dutton-Swift and Philip Spencer-Smith were retreating from the Black Horse, he was on the telephone to the Crunchy Choc people. The pneumatic drills were in full blast. If he had given a moment's clear thought to the situation, Dimmock would have realized that it was not necessary for him to raise his voice on the telephone above the noise of the drills. As it was, he was bellowing so hard into the instrument that Crunchy Choc could not understand what he was saying. He assumed that this was because the drills were drowning him, and therefore shouted louder than ever.

'I looked at a lay-out this morning . . . I say, I looked at a lay-out this morning . . . but I said it wasn't good enough . . . *wasn't good enough* . . . dead wrong for Chunky Choc products . . . I said Chunky Choc products – what d'you think I'm talking about? Rockets? . . . Not properly aimed at your public . . . I say, *not properly aimed at your public* . . . not rockets – why should I ring you up about rockets? . . . I say, *why should I ring you up about rockets?* . . . Oh, for God's sake . . . I'll ring you later . . . I say, *I'll ring you later –* '

He put down the telephone and passed a handkerchief over his glistening forehead. At his elbow were some sandwiches and a glass of milk. In an abstracted worried fashion, he drank a little milk and nibbled at a sandwich. He still could not help glancing suspiciously at the large cupboard on the opposite wall. It looked blank enough, just a plain office cupboard for books and files that were better out of sight, and yet he had a fancy that it was jeering at him.

And then he saw the rat. It was a big brown rat, and somehow, without the doors being opened, it had come out of the cupboard. It moved forward about a yard, sat up on its hind legs, looked at him, and then made a noise that sounded like *He-he-he!*

This was too much. Furious, Dimmock jumped up, hurled a notebook at the rat and missed it by a couple of feet or so. The rat went *He-he-he!* again, and then popped back into the cupboard.

'Peggy,' he shouted into his box, 'come in – quick.' He tried another sandwich but found it distasteful, perhaps flavoured with rat.

'Peggy,' he began indignantly, 'we've got rats here.'

'I've tried to tell you that,' said Peggy. 'I could name two of them, Mr Dimmock – downright disloyal to the firm –'

'No, I mean real rats. I've just seen one. Came out of that cupboard.'

'Oh – surely not, Mr Dimmock.'

'I tell you it did,' Dimmock shouted. 'A big fat brown rat – cheeky as hell. It stood there, laughing at me. When I threw a pad at it and missed, it laughed at me again. Then it went back into the cupboard. What d'you think of that?'

Peggy shook her head at him. 'I think you ought to go home, Mr Dimmock.'

'Go home? What are you talking about?'

'Your health comes first, Mr Dimmock.'

'I dare say, but what's that to do with rats?'

'I don't think you ought to make yourself stay here and try to attend to business, Mr Dimmock. I know how conscientious you are – we all do – but business isn't everything. Wouldn't you like me to send for the car and then ring up Mrs Dimmock?'

'No, I wouldn't,' said Dimmock angrily. 'Just because I saw a rat!'

'Not just the rat,' said Peggy beginning to sound and to look tearful. 'You said you saw a dwarf.'

'Well, I *did* see a dwarf.'

'And you said *he* went into the cupboard too.'

'That'll do, Peggy,' said Dimmock, suddenly from a height of dignity. 'You get on with your work and let me get on with mine.'

'Yes, Mr Dimmock.' She turned away.

'And tell 'em next time I don't want sandwiches that taste like sawdust.'

She stopped in the doorway, to turn and look at him reproachfully. 'Oh – Mr Dimmock – it's not the sandwiches – it's *you*.'

As soon as she had gone, he went over to the cupboard and opened it cautiously. It was just as it had been before, solidly packed with books and files, not offering enough free space even for a rat. After regarding it thoughtfully for a moment, he closed the doors and walked slowly back to his desk. He picked up the glass of milk and a sandwich he had not tried before, turned his back on the room and stared out of the window. The brown young fiends with the pneumatic drills, all healthy and happy, had formed a group, laughing together, getting ready for their next attempt to shake the district to pieces. Then a noise in the room brought him round. A very beautiful girl, expectant and gay and dressed in some sort of medieval costume, was standing there, smiling at him. It flashed across his mind that she too might have come out of the cupboard, but hastily he dismissed the ridiculous notion.

'Now – what's this?' he said gruffly.

'It's me.' She smiled at him sweetly. 'Who are you?'

'Seeing this is my room, I ought to be asking *you* that. However, as you're new, I'll tell you. I'm Mr Dimmock, one of the directors here. And though you look very nice, my dear, you must understand we can't have models in costume roaming about just as they like. We'd soon be all at sixes and sevens.'

'What sixes and sevens?'

'You know what I mean. What are you doing here?'

'I'm looking for Sam.'

'Oh – the Damosel Stockings job,' said Dimmock, rather relieved. 'Well, Sam *was* here, but then he went off. I've sent Anne Dutton-Swift and Philip Spencer-Smith to bring him back, so he oughtn't to be long. As soon as he comes, you'd better pose for him again.'

'I think I love Sam,' the girl said dreamily.

'You're not the first, so take it easy. What's your name, dear?'

'I am Princess Melicent.'

'Doesn't surprise me,' said Dimmock. 'We'd the granddaughter of a Russian grand-duchess working for us, last year. And an Italian *contessa*. Make good models too, you aristocratic girls – it's the training, I suppose.'

'I don't know what you are saying,' Melicent began. But then the drills started. She was terrified and put her hands over her ears.

'I ought to have warned you, my dear,' said Dimmock, when they stopped. 'It's only the pneumatic drills.'

'Why do you have such terrible things?' Melicent cried reproachfully. 'We don't have them in real life.'

'In what?'

'In real life. Have you seen Master Marlagram, the enchanter?'

'Never heard of him. What I did see was a big brown rat that either went *He-he-he!* or I'm barmy.'

'That was Master Marlagram. He said he'd transform himself before he saw you.'

Dimmock stared at her and began breathing deeply and noisily. 'Just hold it, Princess, will you?' He spoke into his box: 'Peggy, I want you in here – sharp.' Then he looked at Melicent again. 'When my secretary comes in, just tell her what you've just told me. She thinks I ought to go home and lie down.'

'You are sick?' said Melicent, going closer and regarding him sympathetically. 'You have a kind face, but it is sad. Perhaps you should go home and lie down.'

'I hate lying down.' He looked at Peggy, who had just come in. 'Peggy, this is Princess – er – Melicent – who's been posing for Sam. Now, Princess, you just tell Peggy what you told me – about Master Who's-it – '

'Alison,' said Melicent, staring at Peggy. 'How did *you* come here?'

'Well, how did *you* know my other name's Alison? Oh – you must be the girl my cousin Audrey mentioned to me. But you oughtn't to have come in here. By the way, your nose is a bit – haven't you got your compact?'

'Compact?'

Peggy produced hers and opened it.

'Oh – how wonderful!' cried Melicent, staring at it in an ecstasy. 'Better than anything in real life. I must have one of these before Sam comes back.'

'I'll show you where we girls go,' said Peggy, and took her out.

Bewildered, Dimmock watched them go, and then opened one drawer after another until finally he found a flask. He poured some of its contents into the milk, and began sipping the mixture, still darting suspicious glances at the cupboard. He had just drained the glass when Anne Dutton-Swift and Philip Spencer-Smith marched in.

'Well, did you get Sam?'

'No, D.D.,' said Phil. 'We went to the Black Horse pub – his local – and found a mad barmaid there.'

Anne was giggling. 'She said Sam had gone through the wall – '

'To find a princess in a Portuguese lighthouse.' Phil laughed.

'It's true, D.D., we're not making it up.'

'Well, Sam's model is here,' said Dimmock. 'All dressed up. Very good-looking girl too. She says she's a princess – ' The telephone rang. 'Dimmock speaking. . . . Spencer-Smith? Yes, he's here.' He held out the receiver. 'Television people for you. Flapping again.'

'Spencer-Smith here. Yes? . . . she's *what*? . . . Well, I warned you to have some other girl lined up, didn't I? . . .' As he listened to the apology at the other end, he saw Melicent come in, and brightened up at once. 'I know . . . I know . . . but now you're asking me at the last minute. . . . All right, I think I have somebody. Hold everything, chaps.' He put down the receiver and looked at Dimmock. 'D.D., I'm in a jam. SOS. Can I take this model of Sam's? Okay?' He turned to Melicent. 'Lovely little job for you on the telly, dear – can do?'

'What are you saying?'

'No time to stop and explain, dear. Tell you on the way.'

'Will I see Sam?'

'Don't think so – but he might see and hear *you*. Let's go, ducky.'

But Melicent turned at the door to address Dimmock: 'If Master Marlagram the enchanter comes back, tell him what has happened to me. And don't think you can't talk to him because he looks like a brown rat.'

Anne watched her go and then stared at Dimmock. 'D.D., *what* did that girl say?'

He replied in a kind of controlled fury, 'Can't you understand a perfectly simple request, Anne? She said I must talk to Master Marlagram the enchanter even if he looks like a brown rat.' Then he began shouting. 'And don't start arguing about it. Just leave it.'

'All right,' said Anne. 'But where did that girl come from?'

'Out of the cupboard.' And as Anne was about to say something, he shouted, 'I said, "Leave it, leave it" – you can hear me, can't you? Well, when I say "Leave it", I mean "Leave it".' He glared at his desk, and suddenly noticed something. 'Now, who did this?' He picked up a large calendar and hurled

it across the room, where it landed face upwards: *June 31st.*
Then Peggy came in.

'Mrs Dimmock's coming to take you home. And Dr Jarvis
is on his way to see you, Mr Dimmock.'

'Oh – Christmas crackers!' The telephone rang, and the des-
pairing Dimmock snatched up the receiver. 'Who? – Mum's
Chum Products? Look – I'm sick of hearing about that muck
of yours.' He slammed down the receiver.

'D.D., have a heart,' Anne cried in alarm. 'It's one of our
best accounts.'

'He's not himself, Miss Dutton-Swift,' said Peggy. 'I'm sure
Dr Jarvis – '

'Oh – Jiminy Jorkins!' Dimmock, about to explode now,
began drumming on his desk. 'There must be some way out
of all this – '

'*He-he-he!*'

'Did you hear that?'

'Something squeaking,' said Anne. 'But, honestly, D.D. –
we'll have to explain to Mum's Chum – '

'Shut up. Now – listen.'

'*He-he-he!*'

'Why don't you take your collar off, Mr Dimmock?' said
Peggy. 'And if you took your shoes off, you could lie down – '

'Shut up.' Purple in the face now, Dimmock got up and
glared around, like a bull at bay.

'Try the cupboard,' said the squeaky voice. '*He-he-he!*'

'All right, by thunder, I will!' shouted Dimmock. And he
ran round and dived clean through the cupboard.

'After him – after him,' cried Peggy wildly. 'We can't let
him go like that. Come on.'

'Now then, Mr Dimmock,' said Dr Jarvis importantly as
he marched in. 'What's this I hear?' But what he saw was
Anne Dutton-Swift, following Peggy, disappearing into the
cupboard. He hesitated a moment, then moved majestically
across to the cupboard and threw open the doors. But all he

saw were shelves crammed tight with books and files. And all he heard, after a bewildered moment, was the earth-shaking chorus of pneumatic drills.

CHAPTER SIX

Sam in Trouble

Thinking it over afterwards, Sam decided that going from
Peacock Place to Peradore had been like travelling very fast
and waking up, both at the same time. Somewhere on the
way, if you could call it a way, he had lost both Malgrim and
Skip Plunket, and he was not feeling too cheerful when he
began climbing a lot of steps in what was obviously a castle.
Moreover, Sam liked to eat a substantial lunch – none of your
sandwiches and salads but something like steak-and-kidney
pud or baked jam roll – and it was hours since he had swallowed a hasty breakfast, and now he was feeling hungry. He
was of course longing with all his heart to find the exquisite
Princess Melicent, but this did not mean that he had no desire
whatever for Lancashire hot-pot, Irish stew, boiled beef and
dumplings. But not a whiff of anything of the sort came his
way. However, at the top of the steps, somebody was playing
a lute, and once he had barged in Sam felt he ought to stay
and listen.

'Thanks very much,' he said. 'Let's have another one, shall
we?'

The lute-player rose, smiled, bowed.

'Now – wait a minute,' Sam went on. 'I heard a thing the
other night on the air – you'll probably know it. Oh – yes –
"The Black Knight Hath My Heart".'

'Bah!' said the lute-player, scowling. He picked up his
instrument and stalked past Sam.

'Did you say *Bah*?' Sam called after him. 'I've often read it,
but I've never heard it before.'

Left to himself, Sam decided that he might as well explore
this tower, if only to try to forget how hungry he was. Push-

ing aside some rather moth-eaten hangings, he walked slap into a magnificent-looking red-head in an emerald green dress. Her smile was almost an illuminated Welcome.

'How doth my fair lord,' she began, 'after so much hath befallen him?'

Sam did his best. 'Fair gentlewoman – er – I am come to no harm – but – er – am yet amazed.'

'Fair sir, sithen ye seek adventure, to win prowess, ofttimes must ye stand amazed.'

This was hard going. 'Noble damsel – er – ye say sooth. Er – what name – er – '

'I am Lady Ninette.' She curtsied, smiling away. 'And among my kindred are many great lords and noble ladies.'

'Fair Lady Ninette,' said Sam, rather desperate now, 'I am called Sam – and the name of my family is Penty. And my kindred – to speak truth – are no great shakes.'

'And you are no great shakes at this kind of dialogue, are you, Sam?'

'Oh – we needn't keep it up? Good! By the way, Lady Ninette, as you were kind enough to ask me how I was feeling, I must confess I'm feeling very hungry.'

'I was sure you would be,' said Ninette. 'Well, everything's ready. This way. I'm hungry myself, Sam. I waited for you, knowing you were coming. Wasn't that nice of me?'

'It certainly was, Lady Ninette. I was just about to say so. By George, what a spread!' There seemed enough food for a dozen people, though clearly it had been set out only for the two of them.

'I'm afraid I hadn't time to order anything very special,' said Ninette carelessly. 'But you may like the cold peacock and swan, the honey-and-almond castle – and the goose pasty is supposed to be rather good.'

'A smashing lunch.'

'Do sit down, Sam. Let me give you some wine. Help yourself to the goose pasty.'

After eating and drinking heartily for some minutes, Sam felt he might risk a question or two. 'By the way, Ninette, what age are we in here?'

'What age?'

'Yes. What king's reigning?'

'Arthur is still High King.'

'Of course – all Arthurian. Legendary really. Then I suppose everything is still in full swing – knights, enchanters, dragons, giants – '

Ninette looked surprised. 'Naturally. The usual Arthurian way of life. Who rules your mythical kingdom, Sam?'

'Nominally, a queen, Elizabeth the Second,' Sam told her. 'But actually, the executive committees of the Conservative and Labour Parties, the Trades Union Congress, the Federation of British Industries, the Bow Group, the Fabian Society – '

Ninette laughed so much she spilt some wine on the roast swan. 'Sam darling, do stop it, I know you're making it up. Now let's be serious and have some cosy plot talk. I'm very anxious to know how Master Malgrim brought you here. I haven't seen him since he asked me to be ready to receive you, Sam.'

'Well, we were through almost in a flash,' said Sam. 'I felt a bit dizzy, of course – Private Bar of the Black Horse to Peradore in one move – and then I found that Malgrim had disappeared, and with him a rather rum bloke, Captain Plunket, who'd insisted upon coming along. No idea where they are. Not counting a lute-player who took offence, you're the first person I've had any talk with here, Lady Ninette.'

She looked at him out of the corners of her long green eyes. 'But rather a nice person, don't you think, Sam?'

'Delicious!' He hesitated. 'But – er – something was said about a Princess Melicent.'

'Oh – Sam!' She sounded disappointed.

'Said the wrong thing, have I?'

'You're not a snob, are you, Sam?'

'Not in the least.' He gave her an apologetic grin. 'But I understood from Malgrim that the girl I painted was a Princess Melicent, and – well, you know how it is, Ninette – that's the one I'm looking for.'

'Is she any fairer in your sight than I am?' Ninette demanded haughtily. 'Methinks – '

'No, don't let's get back to that stuff. As a matter of fact I've never seen her as clearly as I'm seeing you – and you're certainly a devastatingly seductive piece – I beg your pardon.'

'Not at all. I like it. More wine, Sam?' She filled his tankard again.

'Thank you, Ninette,' said Sam, who was beginning to feel a bit swimmy. 'You're both adorable girls, I see that. Different types, that's all. But it's Princess Melicent I'm trying to find.'

'She's a ninny,' said Ninette.

'Perhaps I need a ninny.' Sam grinned at her, then took a hearty swig of wine – a roughish red, not bad at all.

'Don't be ridiculous.' She gave him a hard look. 'Now *I'm* intelligent and rather wicked.'

Sam could not think of a reply to that remark, so he let it go. There was silence between them for about half a minute. Ninette now leant forward. 'Do you know the Macbeths?'

'I know *of* them,' said Sam.

'I've a cousin in Scotland who knows them very well. A few years ago, the Macbeths were nothing – just Army people. Look at them now. All *her* doing. *She* has the brains – the determination – the drive.'

'You wait,' said Sam grimly.

'Of course you couldn't give me Scotland. But here too it's the clever and rather wicked women who have all the fun. Look at Morgan le Fay, Guenevere, Nimue, Etarre, the Queen of Orkney. It's only clever women and enchanters who can *plot*.'

'In our world,' said Sam, 'we don't need wicked plots any

more. We can all do ourselves in, very nicely, with science and progress. But tell me about the enchanter situation here – I'm not very clear about it.'

'It's rather fascinating,' Ninette began. 'There are two enchanters – Malgrim, the one I'm working with, and his old uncle, Marlagram. Now Marlagram outwitted Malgrim, and took Melicent to find you. '

'Then what am I doing here?'

'Well, you see, Malgrim, who's terribly clever, then out-witted his uncle by bringing you here before poor Melicent could find you. And now you're here, but she's there.'

'And we're both of us in the wrong worlds,' said Sam indignantly. 'I call that a bit much.'

Here he was interrupted by the herald: 'His Royal Majesty – King Meliot of Peradore – High Lord of Bergamore, Mar-ralore and Parlot – Overlord of Lancington, Low Moss and Three Bridges!'

The trumpets sounded, and King Meliot came bustling in. He was attended by an aged counsellor, Malgrim in his magnificent black-and-silver signs-of-the-zodiac costume, and two soldiers. The King looked as if he had had an enormous lunch and too much wine, had fallen asleep but had been wakened too early, and was now not very clear about any-thing and in a thoroughly bad mood. Sam took a poor view of him.

'What's happening here?' the King shouted. He pointed to Sam. 'Who's this fella? No, tell us later. Point is – where's our dwarf?'

'He's here, sire,' said Ninette. 'Brought back by Master Malgrim, the enchanter.'

'Oh – that fella. Don't trust him.' King Meliot now pointed at Malgrim. 'Who's this fella?'

'*I* am Master Malgrim, Your Majesty.'

'Dam' confusing, all this. But don't think we won't straighten it out,' the King shouted.

'God bless our good King Meliot,' cried the aged counsellor, in a high quavering voice. 'Hip – hip – "'

'Hurray!' cried the two soldiers. But they sounded as if they had had to do this too often.

'All right, that'll do.' The King, glaring, now pointed to Sam. 'Now what about this fella?'

'Not one of your subjects, sire,' said the aged counsellor.

'We can see that for ourselves,' said the King sharply. 'Fella

isn't properly dressed. One of these fellas from Lyonesse or Cameliard – eh? Hasn't had himself announced. Not presented any credentials. And now being given a dam' great lunch at our expense.' He peered at the table, and then went closer. 'That goose pasty is reserved for our royal table. What the blue blazes is it doing here? What goes on? Fella turns up from nowhere – no credentials, not even properly dressed – and our best wine's poured into him, and he's allowed to wade into our best goose pasty. *Who is he?*'

'A dangerous young man, Your Majesty,' said Malgrim smoothly. 'He came seeking Princess Melicent. He's the man she saw in my magic mirror – Sam.'

'Sam? She said he didn't exist in real life. Character in

mythology, legend, folk-lore, we understood. No, this must be some other fella. What's your name?'

'Sam. And I'm the fellow she meant. We're in love. At least I hope so. I know I am.'

This declaration sent King Meliot into a fury. 'Stares us in the face – improperly dressed – full of our best pasty – and now tells us he's in love with our only daughter! By Cock and Bull, this makes our blood boil.'

'Perhaps a statement later by a Castle spokesman – ' the aged counsellor began.

'Nonsense! Melicent! Melicent!' the King shouted. When no reply came, he looked at Ninette. 'Where is she?'

'Not here, sire. She went to look for him – Sam.'

'Oh – she did, did she? Well, tell her from us where she'll find him. In our deepest dungeon. Take him away, you men. Knock him senseless if he tries to escape.' There was a struggle, but the two soldiers were soon able to remove Sam. When they had gone, the King looked round and then grabbed the goose pasty from the table.

'There's going to be a devil of a row too about this goose pasty,' he told Ninette. 'You've not heard the last of this, girl. But you've *seen* the last of it.' He took a large bite out of the pasty and went bustling out, followed shakily by the aged counsellor.

'Sit down and have some wine, Master Malgrim,' said Ninette, smiling at him. 'I must say, I adore this – I mean being a conspirator in a plot. And you've been wonderfully clever.'

'It's neat, I think,' said Malgrim, accepting the wine. 'Though you mustn't underestimate Uncle Marlagram. But so far I'm at least one move ahead of him. Sam's here – in the deepest dungeon. She's there.'

'Still in Sam's world? Marvellous!'

'Yes, and very soon they're *putting her on the air.*'

'What does that mean, Master Malgrim? What air?'

'It's a form of enchantment they have,' said Malgrim carelessly. 'Drab stuff. My uncle and I wouldn't put our names to such dreary drivel. And I don't think Melicent will enjoy being on the air any more than Sam will enjoy his dungeon – *ha-ha*!'

Ninette looked at him admiringly. 'Aren't you wicked?'

CHAPTER SEVEN

Melicent is on the Air

In the television studio, Burton Chiddleworth, chairman of the *Discussion For You* programme, kept looking anxiously at his watch.

'Everything's under control, isn't it?' said Philip Spencer-Smith. 'I realize that girl I've brought you probably hasn't a clue. But you must admit she looks wonderful.'

'I'm not worried about her,' said Chiddleworth. 'But our rural character – Josiah Hooky – hasn't turned up yet, and we're on the air in ten minutes. He's been late before – and of course he's always tight – but this time he's cutting it too fine. Blast the man. I was against having him on the programme from the start, but Rupert and Nancy insisted on our having a rural character – hello, who's this?'

A little old man with a long beard, wearing a smock and carrying a pitchfork, was making his way towards them, moving so fast that he almost seemed to be capering.

'You'll get no Josiah Hooky this afternoon, mister,' he said, looking and sounding as if he were filled with malicious glee. 'So I'm taking his place. *He-he-he!* Name's Marlagram. Come up from the country too – you can see that. *He-he-he!*'

'I can't,' said Burton Chiddleworth. 'In that corny rig-out you look like somebody left over from the last Number Two Touring Company of *The Farmer's Wife*. Are you really from the country or from the back pages of *Spotlight*?'

'Oi be prapper country-bred, maister,' cried Marlagram. 'An' all ready now when you are. *He-he-he!*' He went off to talk to the Princess, who welcomed him eagerly.

'I'm an intuitive,' said Chiddleworth darkly. 'And some-

thing tells me, Spencer-Smith old man, that this afternoon's *Discussion For You* is going to be a stinkeroo. Mrs Shiny never stops gabbling. Poor Ted Gizzard gets entangled in his polysyllables. Your beautiful dumb blonde probably won't utter. And now we've got this king of the trolls. Somebody'll have to take that smock and pitchfork away from him. My guess is that he's really twenty-two years of age and just got his first part at the Arts Theatre. All right, Charlie,' he called. 'We'll get in our places.'

Mrs Shiny was a large fatuous woman, with a lot of nose and bosom. Ted Gizzard was a bony, stubborn type who had educated himself so thoroughly in committee language that he could hardly speak ordinary English at all. Watching the four of them take their places on each side of Burton Chiddleworth, the Princess next to Ted Gizzard, Marlagram next to Mrs Shiny, Philip began to feel anxious himself. The girl was stunning to look at, but nothing he had heard her say yet had made much sense. And this little Marlagram chap, though he must be at least eighty, was winking and nodding and chuckling and rubbing his hands together, in a kind of gleeful senility.

'Good afternoon,' said Chiddleworth, smiling at one-and-a-quarter million housewives, to say nothing of countless school-children with mumps and measles. 'Welcome once

again to our *Discussion For You* programme. On my right – an
old favourite on this programme – is Mrs Shiny, who as you
all know is President of the Housewives' and Homemakers'
Guild. And next to her, taking the place of Josiah Hooky,
who is indisposed, is Mr – er – Marlagram, ready to give us
the rural and agricultural view of things. Over on my left
here – another old favourite and a well-known figure in the
Trade Union movement – Ted Gizzard, General Secretary of
the Copper Scaling and Brass Layabouts' Union. And next to
him – another newcomer – a very charming addition to our
panel, I think you'll agree – now enjoying a successful career
as a model here in London – Princess Melicent.'

'I only came to find Sam,' Melicent announced firmly.
'Where is he?'

'Tell you later, girl,' said Marlagram. *'He-he-he!'*

'Yes, yes,' said Chiddleworth hastily, 'that's very very interesting – and I hope we'll get round to it. Now, Mrs Shiny
– first question to you. A regular viewer asks us this: "What
new opportunities should be given to women?" Mrs Shiny?'

'Well, I speak as a housewife and homemaker,' said Mrs
Shiny, with colossal self-importance, 'because, as you know,
I'm President of the Housewives' and Homemakers' Guild,
the largest and most influential association of housewives and
homemakers in the country. And speaking *as* a housewife and
homemaker, I would say that every possible new opportunity
ought to be offered to women, especially in their capacity as
housewives and homemakers.'

'Jolly good,' said Chiddleworth. 'Thank you very much,
Mrs Shiny. Ted Gizzard?'

'Without committing myself beyond further disputation,'
said Gizzard very slowly, 'I think I might reply to that particular question, without prejudice of course – '

'Get on with it, lad,' cried Marlagram.

'I say, without prejudice of course,' continued Gizzard,
'but venturing to speak not only for the Copper Scaling and

Brass Layabouts but also for the whole consolidated Trade
Union movement as it is constituted today – I would say yes
and no, perhaps and perhaps not – having regard to the fact
that circumstances alter cases.'

'Splendid. Thank you, Ted Gizzard. Now what's the coun-
tryman's view of this important question, Mr Marlagram?'

'Eggs butter cheese, splish splash splutter and splosh, milk
in the dairy, milk in the pail, drippity, droppity, drappity drum,
take the cows out, bring the cows in, pigs in the barley, geese
in the grass.' Marlagram was gabbling at a fantastic speed,
with an earnestly thoughtful look on his face. 'On the whole
no – but sometimes yes – specially in April and September,
leaving out all Fridays.'

'I see,' said Chiddleworth, who certainly didn't. 'Now, Princess Melicent, what new opportunities do *you* want?'

'I want Sam,' said Melicent firmly.

'Just been taken to the dungeon,' said Marlagram.

'The dungeon?'

'The deepest – *he-he-he!* But don't worry, it'll work out.'

'Mr Chairman,' Mrs Shiny began, 'I must say – '

'Yes, yes – very interesting,' said the desperate Chiddleworth. 'You mean that Sam will provide the new opportunities, Melicent?'

'Don't call me Melicent,' she told him severely. 'You're not
one of my friends.'

'Speaking as a housewife,' said Mrs Shiny, 'and as President – '

'Don't interrupt,' said Melicent sharply. 'Master Marlagram,
are you sure Sam's in the dungeon?'

'Point of order, Mr Chairman,' said Ted Gizzard. 'In my
opinion the item on the agenda does not involve any substi-
tution of the particular for the general, the personal for the
impersonal – '

'Well of course there's something in that,' said Chiddleworth hastily. 'But now – '

'Another point of order, Mr Chairman,' said Marlagram. 'In my opinion – *he-he-he!* – sensational effervescence repudiates illimitable constitutions favouring complicated verbosities.'

'I didn't catch that,' said Gizzard.

'And what are your impressions so far of London, Princess Melicent?' asked Chiddleworth, mopping his forehead.

'If it isn't real,' said Melicent earnestly, 'and you've made it all up, then why have you made it so horribly ugly and noisy, and why do people look so anxious or angry or sad? Unless of course it's all an evil enchantment.'

'I beg your pardon – a *what*?'

'*An evil enchantment.*'

'I've spent thirty years in the Trade Union movement,' said Gizzard, 'and in my opinion – '

'Oh – be quiet!' Melicent looked across and saw that Marlagram's chair was now empty. A large brown rat was ambling across the floor. 'Master Marlagram, Master Marlagram, where are you going?'

'To have a word with Sam. *He-he-he!*'

'Take me with you.'

'Later, my dear. Be in the Black Horse about six o'clock. *He-he-he!*'

'He-he-he!' This came as a desperate echo from Chiddleworth, who felt not unreasonably that he was losing control of the programme. 'Very very interesting – and we do wish them all the best of luck.'

'Certainly,' said Gizzard.

'Well now – the next question comes from a regular viewer in Surbiton, who wants to know if there will be more women than men in the near future and, if so, how. Mrs Shiny?'

'Speaking as a housewife,' said Mrs Shiny, 'and on behalf of many thousands of responsible British housewives, who are all deeply concerned about the near future, I would say possibly and possibly not – but that it's difficult to say exactly how. Don't you agree, Mr Gizzard?'

'I do to a limited extent, and I don't to a much less limited and larger extent, though mind you I don't want to be dogmatic and categorical. But we in the Trade Union movement – '

'I think this is silly,' said Melicent, getting up. 'And I'm going. Good afternoon.'

All the way back to the office, Philip Spencer-Smith explained how Melicent's behaviour on the programme might keep Wallaby, Dimmock, Paly and Tooks out of television for the next two years. Melicent, who was thinking about Sam in the dungeon, did not even pretend to listen. He said he would talk to Anne Dutton-Swift first, before telling Dimmock what had happened. But Anne was not there, and nobody knew where she was. Peggy was not there, and nobody knew where she was. And, to crown all, Dimmock had gone, and nobody had seen him go.

'I must say, this is a bit much,' he told Melicent. 'First, Sam – '

'I know where Sam is,' said Melicent unhappily. 'He's in our dungeon at Peradore. Didn't you hear that rat telling me? That was Master Marlagram.'

'I could of course,' said Philip carefully, 'be going quietly out of my mind. I wonder if Dr Jarvis is still around.'

But Dr Jarvis, it seemed, after a lot of muttering about a cupboard, had gone to consult a colleague in a psychiatric clinic.

'You'll have to take me to the Black Horse,' said Melicent.

'Suits me,' said Philip. 'As soon as they're open, ducky. But we needn't go so far, if it's a drink you want.'

'It isn't. I want Sam.'

'But you said he was in your dungeon, whatever that means.'

'If I don't go to the Black Horse I won't be able to see Sam in the dungeon – '

'For Pete's sake, turn it up, will you?' Philip shouted, throwing the Mum's Chum lay-out across the room.

Melicent burst into tears.

CHAPTER EIGHT

Sam in the Dungeon

It really was the deepest dungeon. The two soldiers had taken Sam down to the ordinary dungeon level, had then opened a door about a foot thick, pushed him down some slippery and worn stone steps, then closed the foot-thick door on him. What little light there was came from one small window, high up and well out of reach. It was a loathsome hole. It had the same peculiar sad smell that old magazines have, piled up in the corner of an attic. Sometimes Sam sat on a block of damp mossy stone, sometimes on the bottom step but two. From a dark corner, which he did not propose to explore, came the sound of dripping water and some sloshy noises that suggested creatures of some sort. The whole thing was no joke at all. Unfortunately, he had decided that in the first two minutes, and for the next eighty or ninety minutes there did not seem to be anything else to decide. He had eaten so much at lunch, and drunk so much wine, that in any sensible kind of place he could have fallen asleep, but down here it was too dank and slimy. So he just yawned and cursed.

Finally, the door above was opened, bringing some light at last. The two soldiers came down the steps, apparently very pleased with themselves.

'Bread,' the first soldier announced, offering Sam a loaf.

'Water,' said the second one, putting down a jar.

'Which is what you're on, chum.'

This set them guffawing. Sam looked at them with disgust. 'I don't see the joke.'

'Ar – we're just kiddin' you, see, chum,' said the first soldier. 'That's your official ration, as per dungeon regulations. But Fred an' me's soft-'earted, aren't we, Fred?'

'That's right, Jack.'

'So look what we won you out of the cook'ouse, chum.'
And he produced a parcel crammed with slices of beef and
ham and pasty ends. 'Start in on that lot – an' never mind
sayin' thank you.'

'Just get stuck into it, Mac,' said the second soldier,
Fred.

'No, thanks,' said Sam.

'What's the matter with you?' Jack demanded. 'Lovely
grub. What you turnin' your nose up at it for?'

'No bleedin' gratitude,' said Fred.

'We thought you'd be cryin' your eyes out at the very sight
of it, didn't we, Fred? Now get started. Smashing piece of
underdone beef there, to begin with. Look – '

'I'm sorry, chaps, but I can't eat it.'

'Don't take that attitude, Mac,' said Fred reproachfully.
'Never say die. 'Ave to keep up your strength.'

'That's right,' said Jack. 'You might be out of 'ere in a few
months. I've known it 'appen. So don't mind us – just get it
down, chum.'

'How can I when I'm just recovering from a dam' great

lunch?' said Sam. 'You saw it – or what was left of it. I know you mean well, but have some common sense.'

'Mac, if we'd any common, we wouldn't be on this caper.'

A loud voice came down the steps. 'Make way for Sir Skip – the new Captain of the King's Guard.' A tremendously martial figure, wearing full armour and a closed helmet and carrying an immense sword, came clanking down, and the two soldiers scrambled to attention.

'Go wait without,' said the newcomer.

'Without what, Captain?' Both soldiers burst into loud guffaws. 'Not bad – eh, Fred?'

'I don't know 'ow you think of 'em, Jack.'

'Didn't I give you an order?' cried their Captain in a terrible voice. 'Why, you slobbering, pig-faced, muddy-livered, bag-pudding sons of a seacow, do I have to slice off your ears, twist your noses off, chop your thumbs into mincemeat?'

'Nay, nay, Captain.' And the soldiers hurried up the steps.

Once he had taken off his helmet, it was obvious that Plunket, the Old Skip, was very hot and short of breath. He took a long drink out of the jar of water. 'Hellishly hot, this armour, old boy.'

'Cap'n Plunket, are *you* the new Captain of the King's Guard?'

'For the time being, old boy. Had to do some fast talking – and this was the best I could do. Just a stepping-stone.'

'Look what *I* talked myself into.'

'I know, Sam old boy. After the daughter, aren't you? Always tricky. Ever told you what happened to me in Bangkok? Give you the whole story some time. No, not much of a place, this.'

Sam was bitterly indignant. 'Not much of a place! Look at it!'

'I've been in worse, old boy. Twelve of us once in one smaller than this – in Tetuan. Don't worry. I'll have you out of this soon. I'm having supper tonight with this King Meliot, and then I can work something for you, Sam old boy. Ten to one he'll be plastered.'

'And a hundred to one you'll be plastered too, Skipper.'

'Strictly speaking,' said Plunket thoughtfully, 'I've been more or less plastered ever since the abdication of Edward the Eighth. But I can take care of this king. We're very thick already.'

'But how did you work it, Skipper? Why didn't he denounce you for not being properly dressed?'

'Because I pinched some armour first, old boy. Then when we met, he asked me if I came from Camelot, and I said I did. Had I brought him a message to say the meeting was off? So I said I had. He asked me how King Arthur was. Knowing the form, old boy, I said he was looking bronzed and fit and was laughing heartily. Then I recommended myself as Captain of the King's Guard – a new idea to this King Meliot, who's not a bad bloke though on the mean side, I'd say. Dead against you for eating his favourite pasty, he tells me. Not many perks on this job yet, but of course I haven't got going. By the way, old boy, d'you know a fellow called Dimmock – advertising man?'

'Yes, he's my boss. What about him?'

'He's here, old boy.'

'Dimmock? But how did he get here?'

'Something about a rat and a cupboard. Dam' lucky for him we met. Hadn't a clue. Not a very adaptable bloke for an advertising man. Got him under cover up in my room.'

There was a noise at the top of the steps. Hearing it, Plunket immediately jumped up and began shouting ferociously at Sam, 'Why – you impudent rogue – you'll stay here just as long as it pleases His Majesty to keep you here.'

'Sir Skip!' It was King Meliot, peering down the steps. 'Sir Skip!'

'Coming, sire, coming!' Plunket called. Then he whispered, 'Keep your pecker up, old boy. Have you out soon.'

Then, for the King's benefit, he roared, 'Serve you right, you rascal. Coming, sire, coming!'

After Plunket had gone, Sam felt less disconsolate for a quarter of an hour or so, but then the dark mouldy place began to get him down again. Indeed, he felt more relief than alarm when he heard a high chuckling coming from the darkest corner, and a little old man with a long beard suddenly appeared.

'Well, here I am, my boy. *He-he-he!*'

'You're here all right, but who *are* you?'

'Master Marlagram – *your* enchanter – Princess Melicent's enchanter.'

'You've got a nerve,' said Sam indignantly. '*My enchanter!* Look at me. And why did you let Malgrim bring me here, so that Princess Melicent missed me? And what have you done with her?'

'She's all right, lad. Don't worry about her,' said Marlagram, settling down for a chat. 'As for my nephew, Malgrim, he did win a trick this morning, I'll admit. *He-he-he!* Always a hard worker – and moves fast. Trained him myself at one time. The trouble was, I'd an urgent call to Scotland – some old friends, the Weird Sisters – '

'The Macbeth affair, was it?'

'Who's been talking?' Marlagram demanded angrily.

'I'll tell you later,' said Sam. 'But – look here, Mr Marlagram – don't sit there just telling me how smart your nephew is. Family pride's all very well, but if you can't help us – if you feel you're past it – then say so.'

The old enchanter glared at him. '*Past it!* You're talking like a fool, lad. Bar Merlin – and he's retired – I'm the best enchanter between here and Orkney.'

'Then you must be having an off day,' said Sam sulkily.

'*Off day! Past it!* Go on, lad. It only needs a few more words from you, and I'll leave you to it, to get out of this dungeon best way you can.'

'Mr Marlagram, I apologize. By the way, how did you come in? Any good to me?'

'No good to you nor anybody else not in the profession,' said Marlagram sharply. 'We don't serve a twenty years' apprenticeship for nothing, y'know, lad. Well now, let's straighten out a few things. First, Princess Melicent – and a very nice ripe piece too – *he-he-he!*'

'Cut that out. Just get on with the straightening.'

'I left her trying to play a sort of idiot game, under a lot of bright lights,' said Marlagram. 'Told her to be at the Black Horse at six, then I'll bring her back. Just be patient – you'll be seeing her soon.'

'Good. But can one of you get me out of here?'

'Yes, I can. In fact I could do it now.'

'Well, why don't you?'

'Because I don't like working in bits and pieces, any old how, lad. You're an artist – or supposed to be – you ought to be able to understand that. Well, I'm an artist in my own line. When I get you out of here, I want to have a proper design all worked out and be thinking four or five moves ahead. That's where Malgrim, though he's a smart lad, goes wrong. He's all right for a good fast move or two, like this morning, but he's just improvising – and that won't do. I like to have a plan that takes care of everything.'

'And what is it?'

'That's my business, lad.'

'Have a heart,' said Sam. 'It's my business too, isn't it? Here I am – stuck down here.'

'You're a hero, you're brave, aren't you?'

'No,' said Sam. 'If I were, I wouldn't be working for Wallaby, Dimmock, Paly and Tooks. By the way, Dimmock's here.'

'I know – *he-he-he!* Dimmock's part of the plan.'

'Well, what *is* the plan?'

'I'm still working on it. See you later, boy. See you later.'

Then he was no longer there. A last fading *he-he-he!* came from the darkest corner.

Feeling better, in spite of his grumbling, Sam slowly filled his pipe, which somehow he had neglected to do all the afternoon. But then he discovered he had no matches. For a moment he thought of going up the steps, banging on the door to ask for flint and tinder, but then felt it would seem unreasonable. He tried to think tenderly and beautifully about Melicent but found it was impossible now to remember even what she looked like. Instead of Melicent, all he got was a clear image of a bad sculptress called Moya Fetheringhurst, a girl he had disliked for years.

CHAPTER NINE

The Black Horse Again

It was quiet in the Private Bar of the Black Horse, and the fat man, having received his mild and bitter, said so to the barmaid. As she did not reply, he tried again: 'I say, it's quiet.'

'I'm not saying anything.' And the barmaid closed her eyes and folded her mouth away.

'Why's that?'

'Not after this morning, I'm not.' She had opened her eyes as well as her mouth, and now gave the end wall a suspicious look.

The fat man thought this over for a while. Then he found the right question. 'What 'appened this morning?'

'Ask me no questions,' said the barmaid, 'I'll tell you no lies.'

The fat man conceded this. 'That's right.'

After a long pause, the barmaid, almost glaring at him, burst into speech. 'My brother Albert says he saw it done at Finsbury Park Empire one time. Electricity an' mirrors, he says.'

'Saw what done?'

'Vanishing act,' the barmaid replied darkly.

'This morning?'

'This morning. 'Ere.'

'Who did the vanishing?'

'Ask me no questions – '

'That's right,' said the fat man hastily. He swallowed some of his mild and bitter, ruminated for a few moments, then ventured an opinion. 'Turned out nice again.'

'Can't expect anything else,' said the barmaid casually, 'not on the thirty-first of June, you can't.'

He stared at her suspiciously, but the look she gave him was all open innocence. He took out his pocket diary, consulted it anxiously, then stared at her suspiciously again. She returned the same innocent look. The second round between them was about to begin when Malgrim, wearing the same clothes he had worn before here, marched in, brisk and authoritative.

'Oh – my Gawd!' said the barmaid.

'Good evening, madam. Twelve glasses of Benedictine and cold milk, quick as you can.'

'Benedictine and cold milk? Mixed? Twelve glasses?'

'Twelve,' said Malgrim. 'More later, possibly. The bacteriological section of our medical conference is meeting here. Any moment now.'

''Ere, listen,' said the barmaid, still staring at him, 'didn't you come 'ere this morning, drink a whole bottle of creem de menthy – an' then go through the wall?'

'I did – yes,' said Malgrim promptly. 'What of it?'

'*What of it!*' She looked at him in despair, then seemed to make a faint moaning sound as she went to the other end of the bar.

'I fancy,' said the fat man, 'she's a bit off-colour today.'

'So are you, my friend.'

'How d'you mean?'

'Just look at my finger, will you?' Malgrim spoke with such authority, as he raised his finger higher and higher, that it obviously never occurred to the fat man to disobey this order. At the end of twenty seconds, still with his eyes upturned, the fat man, rigid and senseless, might have been a waxworks figure. Malgrim ignored him now and concentrated on the wall. He made signs at it and muttered some spell. There was a sound of rushing wind. The wall opened, but standing there, chuckling triumphantly, was old Marlagram.

'*He-he-he!* Surprised you, didn't I, my boy?'

'Showy, but cheap, as usual, Uncle,' said Malgrim coldly.

'You really ought to retire from serious work, you know. All right for children's parties and that kind of thing – '

'I'll give you children's parties, you conceited young pup!' said Marlagram, coming forward. 'And don't try to ask for any help from Aghizikke and Balturzasas or any o' that group o' demons, 'cos I fixed 'em with a pentacle this afternoon – *he-he-he!*'

'I know you did,' said Malgrim contemptuously. 'Too obvious, my dear Uncle. So I moved, with a cat and bat, to Akibeec and Berkaiac and their group. Want a trial of strength? No, I thought not. No decent strategy, no proper planning. You realize I'm now a move ahead of you?'

'No, I don't, lad.'

'Of course I am. If you go back to Peradore, then you leave me here to meet Princess Melicent.'

'I'm not going to do that, my boy.'

'Very well. Then you stay here, I return to Peradore, and there I'm a move ahead of you. Rather neat, I think. I'll have Merlin's brooch yet – you'll see.' He sauntered towards the opening in the wall.

'You can't close that wall after you, though,' said Marlagram. 'Like to try?'

'Why should I bother? Waste of effort. But the fact remains,' Malgrim said as he passed through the opening, 'I'm a move ahead of you.'

'He is too,' the old man muttered. 'Smart lad, but too pleased with himself. Now – let's see.'

He moved around restlessly, at one moment casually pushing the still rigid fat man out of the way as if he were a piece of furniture. Then a tray with twelve glasses on it made its appearance on the bar counter. The flap underneath the counter opened, and the barmaid, looking dazed, came creeping through. She stood up straight, stared at Marlagram, then at the fat man, then at the opening in the wall.

'Oh – my Gawd!' She closed her eyes, but then, remembering her duty, she opened them to look at Marlagram. ''Ere, could you drink twelve glasses of Benedictine and milk?'

'No,' said Marlagram. 'Never touch milk.'

'Cheery-bye then!' said the barmaid faintly, and went tottering through the opening in the wall, on her way to Peradore.

The old enchanter gave the fat man a tap, saying, 'Wake up,' and then went under the bar counter, to appear behind it. The fat man looked at him, then tried not to look at him.

'I'm 'aving trouble with my eyes,' said the fat man. ''Ere, where's Queenie got to?'

'If you mean the barmaid – he-he-he! – she has a part to play in the Peradore Tournament tomorrow morning, though of course she doesn't know it yet. As for your eyes – they've been looking at nothing, out of nothing.'

''Ow d'you mean?'

'You haven't been alive for years,' said Marlagram. 'What do you drink?'

'Mild and bitter,' the fat man replied, gloomily.

'You've been drowning yourself – he-he-he! What you need is a pint o' dragon's blood. Here!'

Hardly knowing what he was doing, the fat man found himself accepting a pint glass filled with a crimson liquid. 'Ta muchly. New line, isn't it? I don't know what they'll think of next.'

'Who's they?' Marlagram demanded severely.

'Well – you know – '

'I don't know. You don't know. Now drink that – and come to life. Millions of you crawling about, just waiting for free coffins!'

'Well, I'll take a chance.'

'Time you did. And after you've dipped your nose into that dragon's blood, you can tell me what day it is.'

The fat man took a good pull at the crimson liquid. His eyes rolled round for a moment or two, but then a huge grin illuminated his face. 'By crikey – you're right too. So was

Queenie an' that artist chap this morning. It *is* the thirty-first of June.'

'That's more like it,' said Marlagram approvingly.

'Did I ever tell you about that time – ' the fat man began.

'You didn't – *he-he-he!* – and you're not going to. Now then – who's this?'

Philip Spencer-Smith was still complaining to Melicent as they entered the Private Bar. 'I'm not saying you're not a very nice girl, ducky – and probably just right for Sam – but the fact remains you've finished me with television for at least the next two years – '

'Oh – Master Marlagram – I'm so glad to see you,' cried Melicent. 'Hurry up and take me back to real life.'

'We'll be off in a minute – *he-he-he!*'

'What you want,' said the fat man to Philip, 'is a nice drop of this dragon's blood they've got 'ere. Then you won't care if you've finished with the telly for ever. Mister, two pints o' dragon's, please.' He looked at Melicent admiringly. 'That's what you start seein' after a drop o' dragon's. Stick to light ale an' they all look droopy, with dirty black 'air an' chalky faces. Thanks, mister. 'Ave one yourself?'

'Not time,' said Marlagram. 'Off in fifteen seconds from now.'

'Well,' said Philip dubiously, 'try anything once. Cheers!'

'All the best,' said the fat man. They drank together.

'Rather like a Bloody Mary – only more so,' said Philip. Then he stared. No Princess Melicent, no Marlagram, no hole in the wall. 'Er – what – er – I mean to say – how – ' He made a few more vague noises as he looked round, then stared enquiringly at the fat man.

'Turned out nice again,' said the fat man cheerfully.

'Has it?'

'Can't expect anything different, though, can you – thirty-first of June?'

Philip finished his dragon's blood. 'D'you happen to know

Herbert Paly, of Wallaby, Dimmock, Paly and Tooks?' he
heard himself saying. 'Between ourselves, old man, he's a
bigger stinker even than Tooks. Now what about the other
half?'

CHAPTER TEN

King Meliot After Dinner

In a small chamber off the main banqueting hall of the castle, King Meliot was sitting with Captain Plunket and Dimmock, attended only by a cup-bearer. They had dined well and were now drinking hard, keeping the cup-bearer busy. They were also laughing a great deal in a choky and spluttery way, their faces getting redder and redder. They were filled at the moment with the false good-fellowship of middle-aged men who have drunk too much and are trying to forget that morning will ever come.

'We used to know a rather good one,' the King was saying. 'The one about the three chapmen who met in Camelot. We think one of them was an Englishman, another a Scotsman, another an Irishman.' The King laughed heartily. 'Can't quite remember it all, but remind us to tell it to you next time we meet. Cup-bearer!'

'Talking about remembering,' said Plunket, 'I've just remembered something, sire.'

'So have we,' said the King, pointing to Dimmock and frowning at him. 'He's the second fella we've seen today not properly dressed. Other fella's in the dungeon. Wanted our daughter. Damned impudence.'

'I've just remembered,' said Plunket, 'that Dimmock and I have a scheme.'

'Who's Dimmock?' asked the King.

'I'm Dimmock, sire.'

'Then you're not properly dressed, Dimmock. And don't let us have to tell you again. What did you say you had, Sir Skip?'

'A scheme, sire – a plan – a device – an idea. Bags of money in it.'

'Bags of money? Where?'

'In this scheme, sire.'

'We doubt it,' said the King. 'Doesn't seem to us anything in it. Unless of course this fella Dimmock knows more than you do. And where is he?'

'I'm here, Your Majesty. I'm Dimmock.'

'You are, are you?' The King shook his head. 'Well, how far does that take us? No, we've turned down hundreds of ideas better than that. It lacks body. Cup-bearer – fill, fill. Now this wine has some body in it. Your scheme hasn't. That's the difference.' He held up his tankard and squinted at it.

'Your turn,' Dimmock muttered to Plunket. 'I give up.'

'Your Majesty,' Plunket began, impressively, 'I beg leave to drink to your health and happiness and the continued prosperity of your kingdom of Peradore.' He drank, also impressively.

'Very nicely put, Sir Skip, and we're much obliged. But we must point out that our kingdom of Peradore is anything but prosperous. The exchequer, our counsellors tell us, is almost empty.'

'But Dimmock and I, sire, are ready to bring you bags and bags of money –'

'*You* might be, Sir Skip, but is Dimmock? And if he is, let him come and speak for himself.'

'But *I'm* Dimmock.'

The King squinted at him disapprovingly. 'You're not properly dressed. Second fella today. And don't speak unless you're spoken to. In any case, Sir Skip, you ought to have a scheme.'

'We *have* a scheme, Your Majesty.'

'Then why didn't you say so? Why beat about the bush? Cup-bearer.'

'Dimmock, you explain the idea. Your Majesty, Dimmock will outline the scheme.'

'And high time too,' said the King, squinting at Dimmock.

'Well, sire,' said Dimmock, 'where I come from, everybody wants to go somewhere else.'

'Sounds unlikely,' said the King. 'Soon there'd be nobody left.'

'I mean – somewhere else for a holiday.'

'Just for a change,' said Plunket, 'and a rest from their wonderful way of life – '

'Everybody saves money to visit some other country – '

'And we think some of them – the ones with most money – ought to come here – to Peradore – '

'Conducted tours,' cried Dimmock enthusiastically. 'See the castles. See the knights. See the dragons.'

'We'd have to have one of your enchanters working for us, of course,' said Plunket, 'to attend to the transport.'

'But then the money would come rolling in,' said Dimmock.

'To us – kingly *us*, I mean? No, of course not.' The King wagged his head, squinting harder than ever.

'Your Majesty could have a seat on the board,' said Dimmock thoughtfully, 'and a nice holding of the original stock.'

'Boards and stocks? Don't know what you're talking about,' said King Meliot, looking disgusted. 'Where are these bags and bags of money?'

'The money comes into the country,' said Plunket. 'Then you do what our rulers do. As soon as people have money, you take it away from them in taxes.'

'Taxes? Nonsense! A guilder here, a groat or two there – we know about taxes – pooh!'

'But on our plan,' said Dimmock, 'you take half they've got – or three-quarters.'

'You charge 'em for all the castles,' said Plunket. 'Administration and security. For having a roof over their heads. For their clothes and their beds. For the roads and the paths – '

'And for the air they're breathing – eh?' The King laughed derisively.

'Well, that's new,' said Dimmock. 'But you might get away with it. Worth trying.'

King Meliot scrambled to his feet, in a sudden fury. 'Worth trying! Might get away with it! Why, you greedy impudent scoundrels, we'll have you flogged for daring to talk such stuff to us. Cup-bearer, summon the guard. Make haste. Why, you rogues, fellas here have been hanged, drawn and quartered for doing less than you're asking us to do. We wouldn't treat cannibal heathens and one-eyed pigmies in such a scurvily devouring fashion. There isn't a prince in Christendom who'd consent to listen to such evil counsel – and most of 'em would spill your foul brains on the stones.' The two soldiers, Jack and Fred, had now arrived. 'Take these rogues into custody,' the King shouted, 'and if they speak a single word, knock 'em on the head.'

'What, Majesty – our Captain, Sir Skip?'

'He's no longer your Captain. He's a rogue and vagabond, like the other fella. Take 'em away.'

'Ay, ay, Majesty,' said Jack, but he looked dubious. 'Another dungeon job?'

King Meliot was uncertain. 'Well now – let us see – '

It was at that moment that Malgrim and Ninette walked in, not of course by chance, for Malgrim left nothing unplanned. He prided himself, not without reason, on his timing. 'Your Majesty,' he said smoothly, 'may I make a suggestion?'

'And who the devil are you? Oh yes – enchanter fella. Pushing fella – don't overdo it.' Then he noticed Ninette, who was smiling at him. 'Ninette, where's our daughter?'

'I'll explain everything, sire,' said Ninette, in a voice like honey, 'as soon as we're alone. But Master Malgrim – '

'Your Majesty, please allow me to take charge of these prisoners – for the benefit of our art and science.'

'Turn 'em into something, eh?' said the King. 'Not a bad idea. But that doesn't mean you've got a Court appointment now, understand. Off you go, then. Give 'em a hand, Cup-bearer. Lady Ninette can act as cup-bearer.'

'But of course, sire.' Ninette smiled sweetly.

The King watched them go, and then collapsed, seemingly exhausted, into his high chair. 'Fill then, Ninette. And help yourself too, girl.' When he had taken a long drink out of the tankard she gave him, he continued in a rumbling grumbling tone: 'Never an hour's peace these days. King Arthur summons us to Camelot. Then he countermands the summons, sending an absolute rogue of a fella – Sir Skip. Our daughter's half off her head – and now missing. In love with a mythological character. Fellas arriving from nowhere, not properly dressed. Enchanters keep popping in and out without so much as a by-your-leave. Just can't cope with it. Must be getting old.'

'Oh – no, sire, you're in the prime of life.'

'We admit we don't carry our years badly.'

'You're simply rather tired and rather hot,' said Ninette, going closer. 'Allow me, sire.' And she patted his brow with a handkerchief, and then smoothed it with her hand.

'All very well,' said the King, pretending not to enjoy these attentions, 'but where's our daughter?'

'It's a long story,' Ninette began.

'We don't want it then,' said the King. 'Some other time.'

'She's been very naughty, sire. She left our world, looking for this man. Now she's on her way back, with Master Malgrim's uncle – the other enchanter – a horrible old man called Marlagram.'

'What – old *he-he-he* Marlagram? Is he still around? Remember him with Merlin years and years ago. Of course he's a lot older than we are.'

'I should think he's older than anybody is,' said Ninette.

'Well, he could give us at least thirty years. Forty, probably.'

'Of course, sire. And in any case, as my aunt the sorceress used to say, a man is only as old as he feels.'

'She said that, did she? We must remember that. Wish we'd

thought of it. Brilliant original woman, your aunt. Always said so, even at the trial. Fill, girl. Do some cup-bearing.'

'What Your Majesty needs,' said Ninette as she returned with the tankard, 'is somebody like Master Malgrim to relieve you of all the boring routine duties. I know how conscientious you are, but you can't be expected to do everything. It's too much.'

'I should think it *is* too much,' cried an angry voice, making them jump. It was Melicent, and with her was Marlagram.

The King's embarrassment turned to anger. 'Don't talk to us like that. Where have you been? And who's this?'

Marlagram showed no sign of alarm. '*He-he-he!* Surely you remember me, King Meliot?'

'I do now. *He-he-he!* Well, go away, Marlagram,' said the King. 'It's bad enough having your nephew pushing himself forward all the time.'

'A bright lad,' the old man chuckled. 'But mischievous. A tricky plotter but over-confident – you'll see.'

'Is my Sam still in the dungeon?' said Melicent.

'He isn't your Sam,' the King told her angrily, 'but he *is* in the dungeon – and there he's staying.'

'Oh – no, Father – please.'

'And another thing, young woman. We've had enough of your whims and caprices. Tomorrow after the tournament, we announce your marriage – '

'Never – unless it's to Sam.'

'We don't know who the bridegroom will be yet – that's to be decided – but you'll marry him even if we have to lock you up and give you nothing but bread and water.'

'I won't – I won't – I won't – '

'You will,' the King shouted. 'And that's our royal command. Bear witness, Lady Ninette and Master Marlagram, that we have spoken.'

Melicent turned to the old enchanter. 'You remember the brooch that Malgrim wanted – '

'I do. *He-he-he!* We're both after it, of course.'

'It's yours if you help me now,' said Melicent urgently.

'Done!' Marlagram was obviously delighted. 'And notice I never asked for it – *he-he-he!*'

'We wish you wouldn't go on cackling like that,' said the King. 'And what's all this confounded nonsense about a brooch? Whatever it is, we assure you – '

'*Stop, King Meliot!*' Looking strangely impressive now, the enchanter held up a hand. The mellow evening light suddenly changed to a queer green, as if they were all under water. There was a distant rumble of thunder. The girls cried out in alarm.

'None of your old Merlin tricks, Marlagram, please,' said the King uneasily. 'Years out of date, my dear fella. Steady now.'

The green changed to a sinister purple as Marlagram spoke. 'The moment of clear sight, given me under the Seal of Solomon, is with me now, King Meliot of Peradore. Two terrible dangers approach this castle. One is the unknown Red Knight who will challenge all, and overcome all but one, at the tournament tomorrow. The other is a ravening fiery dragon that is even now muttering and smouldering in the wood below. And only he who overcomes the Red Knight can slay the dragon. And it is he who must marry the Princess.'

'Certainly – certainly,' said the King. 'Very reasonable under the circumstances. But, good Master Marlagram, are you sure about the Red Knight and the dragon? There couldn't be any mistake?'

'Mistake?' Marlagram screamed, his face weirdly illuminated in the darkness, his beard a dancing green flame. 'What – you question the moment of clear sight – the Seal of Solomon?' There was a roll of thunder and then a terrible flash of lightning.

'No – no – no,' cried the King, really alarmed now, 'you're quite right. Very reasonable too. We give our word.' He looked around, for the chamber was restored to its evening light, but there was no sign of the enchanter.

'*He-he-he!* I should think so.' The triumphant voice came from nowhere. 'Just another old Merlin trick, King Meliot. Years out of date, no doubt. *He-he-he!*' This last cackle faded away.

'Gone, has he?' said the King, with obvious relief. 'Ninette, fill. One for the road. Well, as we've said many a time, you can't beat the old school of sorcerers when they're really in form. Cranky, expensive, a bit messy, we grant you – but they do let you know exactly where you are.'

'And where are we?' asked Ninette, as she handed him the tankard.

'With a bloodthirsty Red Knight and a fiery ravening dragon on our hands,' said the King cheerfully. 'And if you say it's a bit much, we agree. And now we'd better begin thinking about drafting our proclamation.'

CHAPTER ELEVEN

Meeting in the Dungeon

It was now so dark down there that the two soldiers, Jack and Fred, were carrying torches as well as Sam's supper.

Jack put down a bowl. 'Drop o' broth this time – for a treat.'

'And another loaf,' said Fred.

'Just a loafer, you are, chum,' said Jack. 'Not bad, eh – Fred?'

'You'll kill me yet, Jack.'

'Where's your Captain – Sir Skip?' Sam asked.

'Sir bloody Skip has had it,' Jack told him. 'First we put him under arrest – an' now the enchanter's getting to work on him – *and* on the other bloke.'

'By this time,' said Fred, 'they might be turned into a couple of basset hounds.'

'An' that's a dog's life, chum,' laughed Jack. 'See – Fred, they come like lightnin'.'

'You're a marvel, Jack.'

'I know, Fred. Where's them manacles an' chains?'

'Manacles and chains?' Sam was alarmed. 'I don't want any manacles and chains.'

'It's the rule, see, Mac,' said Fred. 'Like tucking you in for the night.'

'You'll hardly feel 'em, chum,' said Jack, beginning his manacle and chain work. 'What's the broth like?'

'Terrible,' Sam told him. 'What do they make it out of – arrow-heads?'

'You're too choosy, Mac, that's your trouble,' said Fred, helping with the manacles and chains. 'We're all trying to do our best for you – an' look what it gets us.'

'We pass this way only once,' said Jack, making sure the

chains were securely fastened, 'and a few little acts of kindness make all the difference. Both Fred an' me's sensitive –
don't forget that, chum. There! As I said, you'll hardly feel
'em.'

'What – about four hundredweight of iron!' cried Sam.

'Not four, chum. Now you're exaggeratin'. About three,
I'd say.'

'Two an' a half at the most,' said Fred. 'Ever been in the
brig at Caerleon? Strewth – you should see what they put on
you there. Remember that time we were at the depot, Jack?
That time we went square-bashin' with the two armourers?'

'An' we went to the mead-house,' said Jack. 'An' I knocked
out them two redcaps. Ever given yourself a load of mead,
chum? It's murder. Well now, you're all set. An' just to show
you there's no ill-feeling, chum, I'm leavin' you this torch –
I'll put it up here in the bracket. Have a nice night.'

''Appy dreams,' said Fred. They were going up the steps
now.

'Don't I get a blanket or anything?' Sam called up to them.

'What? A warm night like this? You're overdoing it, Mac.'

Sam tried the broth again. It was still terrible. All it tasted
of was pepper, and now his mouth was so dry he found he
could not eat any bread. However, after a few minutes, he
heard the door at the top of the steps being opened again,
and old Marlagram came scurrying down. 'Here I am again,
my boy. *He-he-he!* And here's a real supper.'

'Thanks very much, Master Marlagram.'

'King Meliot's best wine and his favourite pasty – *he-he-he!*'

'There'll be hell to pay if he finds out,' said Sam. 'There
was when I had 'em for lunch.' He bit into the pasty, after
first taking a good swig of wine. 'You brought back Princess
Melicent, of course?'

'Yes, yes – she's here. We've come to a nice little arrange-
ment. She gets what she wants. I get what I want. You couldn't
have it neater.'

'Speak for yourself. I haven't got it neat at all.'

'You haven't got *what*, boy?'

'Sorry – it's this pasty. I say – what happens to me?'

'Well, what do you want to happen to you, lad?' Before Sam could reply, Marlagram went on, 'Now let me tell you something. And don't forget I've been over fifty years more or less in the wish-granting trade. Most people don't get what they want just because they don't know what they want. You can't grant 'em wishes because they haven't any. Now do *you* know what you want, lad?'

'Yes,' said Sam, bringing his face out of the huge tankard.

'Good for you! *He-he-he!* Want to be King of Peradore?'

'God forbid!' Sam was horrified. 'First, I want to get out of this dam' place, naturally. Then I'd like to marry Melicent – tell Wallaby, Dimmock, Paly and Tooks where they can go – try my hand at water-colour landscapes, either this world or the other, don't care which – and do a bit of fishing.'

'No power over anybody?'

'Only water-colours and trout.'

'No riches?'

'I wouldn't know what to do with 'em if I had 'em.'

'You're a born dungeon type, lad. *He-he-he!* But why d'you want to marry Princess Melicent? You've known plenty of girls – pretty girls, clever girls, arty-party-tarty-ever-so-hearty girls – *he-he-he!* – so why come as far as Peradore to marry one?'

'Just a sec,' said Sam, his voice struggling through pasty. 'I need a drink before I answer that one.' He took two hands to the tankard. 'Phew! I'll be tight soon. I want to marry Melicent because she seems to offer me two wonderful qualities I've never found before in the same person – a beautiful strangeness and a loving kindness. A smiling princess – what every man wants. But God knows what she sees in me.'

'God knows,' said Melicent, coming down the steps, 'and I know, Sam darling – but neither of us will ever tell you.'

'She heard everything you said, my boy. *He-he-he!*'

'Oh – my poor sweet – all these chains and things –'

'*He-he-he!*'

She turned fiercely on Marlagram. 'I wish you'd stop making that silly noise and conjure poor Sam out of his chains and things. You can, can't you? Otherwise, I'll run up for a file.'

'Don't think of it,' said Sam. 'It would take us hours and hours.'

'Well?' She looked challengingly at the enchanter.

'Oh – I can do it,' he told her. 'Though chains and manacles are quite tricky and I'm a bit out of practice. Quiet now.' He thought for a moment or two. 'This ought to do it. *Eeny-meeny-miny-mo*. There you are.' And he was right. The manacles and chains fell off with a clatter. Sam was free, and he embraced and kissed Melicent and then shook hands with Marlagram.

'How clever of you, Master Marlagram!' said Melicent. 'I must remember that. *Eeny-meeny-miny-mo*.'

'I've known it for years,' said Sam, 'but never knew it would do anything to chains.'

'Are you having a nice supper, darling?'

'Yes, I am, sweetheart. But what happens now? What's the next move?'

'That's where Master Marlagram's been so very very clever,' said Melicent with enthusiasm.

'And mind you, my nephew – smart lad! – got here first, one move ahead of me.'

'You see, darling,' Melicent continued, 'my father says now I must marry somebody. He's very cross about everything. So Master Marlagram prophesied that there's a terrible Red Knight who's going to challenge everybody at the tournament tomorrow –'

'And a monster fiery dragon's coming too,' said Marlagram, almost licking his lips. 'Might be here already – *he-he-he!*'

Melicent looked at Sam. 'Now my father has agreed that

whoever overcomes them both receives my hand in marriage. And of course that has to be you, darling.'

'Bless you, honeypot.'

'Hasn't Master Marlagram arranged it all cleverly and cunningly?'

'You don't know the half of it,' the old enchanter told her. 'The way I took advantage of being a move behind my nephew – *he-he-he!* Had him working for me without knowing it.'

'Brilliant, I'll bet. What an enchanter!' Sam laughed, though he could not have said why he did. He felt rather light-headed. 'So I go out tomorrow, and pretend to have knocked off a terrible Red Knight and a monster fiery dragon. Marvellous!' He laughed again. 'Well, so long as you give me a few tips about what to say and how to look, I can pretend all that as well as the next man.'

'Just a minute, darling.'

'Sorry – making too much noise. High spirits.' He raised the tankard.

'You see, darling, you won't be *pretending*.'

Sam came spluttering out of his wine. '*What?* You don't mean to say there *is* a Red Knight – and a dragon?'

'But of course, darling.'

'And all you have to do, lad,' said Marlagram, 'is to overcome them – swish-bish-bang-wallop – *he-he-he!*'

Sam stared at him, then at Melicent. 'Here – I say – have a heart.'

'But that's the point, darling. I *have* a heart. And it's all very well talking about every man wanting a smiling princess – very sweet of you, and I'm sure it's true – but of course the one who marries her must have proved himself a hero.'

'What if he isn't a hero?'

'Why bother thinking about that? You *are* a hero. You wouldn't be here if you weren't, darling.'

Sam looked and sounded dubious. 'That may be true – to some extent. But don't forget, this kind of life's quite strange to me. I've never had any experience of tackling Red Knights and dragons.'

'That makes you all the braver, darling.'

'I dare say,' said Sam anxiously. 'But – er – would there be any chance of – let's say – an invisible cloak – or an unbreakable spear – or one of those magic swords that cut through everything – any of the usual heroes' aids?'

'Very sensible, Sam darling. What do you think, Master Marlagram?'

''Fraid not – *he-he-he!* We've left it a bit late, haven't we? An' they all run into money these days.'

'Well,' said Sam, trying to hide his disappointment, 'what about some sort of general enchantment, so that nobody knows exactly what's happening?'

'Then nobody'ud know you're a hero,' said Marlagram.

'And if you aren't a hero, you can't marry me, Sam dear.'

'No, and I can't marry you,' said Sam gloomily, 'if a Red Knight runs me through or a dragon chews me up, can I?'

'That's not the right spirit, lad.' Marlagram was reproachful.

'He doesn't mean it,' said Melicent. 'This horrid dungeon's doing it. Well, you're not staying here, darling. We're putting you into the assistant chief-armourer's room.'

'He'll be there – *he-he-he!* – but he'll be standing in the corner all night. I've made him think he's a mace.'

'So you can have a good night's sleep, darling.'

'I'd have a better night's sleep if I thought I was a mace too.' He began to follow them up the steps. 'What time is the tournament in the morning?'

Melicent called over her shoulder: 'Seven o'clock.'

Sam was horrified. 'A Red Knight at seven o'clock! Why, at that time in the morning I can't face even a fried egg.' He followed them out, any relief he might have felt on leaving the dungeon being lost in dark forebodings.

CHAPTER TWELVE

Sam and the Red Knight

Sam was sitting alone in the marquee-pavilion adjoining the jousting ground. It was a splendid affair, richly decorated and gay with heraldic devices, but Sam was not in the mood to appreciate these things. He was sitting on a stool, half-dressed except for two pieces of leg armour. The rest of his armour, together with his helmet, shield and weapons, was piled up a few feet away. The pavilion had entrances at each end, covered with loose-fitting flaps. Through one of them, along with shafts of brilliant sunlight, were coming all the various sounds of the tournament – the trumpets, the voices of heralds, the clash of arms, the shrieks and laughter and roars of the crowd, already denounced by Sam to himself as a sensation-loving, bloodthirsty mob. There was suddenly an enormous roar, and Sam looked up to see four attendants coming out of the blaze of sunlight, carrying a large and much battered knight, obviously unconscious, through the pavilion, on their way to the first-aid post underneath the Royal Stand. This was the fourth victim of the Red Knight who had been taken through. The trumpets began sounding again, but before the heralds, who might have been toast-masters at City dinners, could begin again, Sam went and hastily closed the flap. As he returned to his stool he saw Lamison, the lute-player, standing just inside the opposite entrance.

'Her Highness Princess Melicent,' said Lamison, 'would fain have a word with thee.'

'Well,' said Sam, moving towards him and speaking in a gloomy tone, 'I would fain have a word with her too – it might be the last.'

Lamison held the flap open for him but did not follow him out. 'Go, fool,' he sneered after him. ' "The Black Knight Hath My Heart" – quotha! The Red Knight hath thy liver, methinks.'

While he was still methoughting in this fashion, Malgrim and Ninette arrived. They were carrying a bundle of armour and weapons similar to the one that Sam had left on the floor.

'Thank you so much, Lamison,' said Ninette. 'Just what we needed.' Lamison, who was going through a bad phase, gave her a sneering acknowledgment and sauntered out.

'Now, you see, my dear Ninette,' said Malgrim, pleased with himself, 'we exchange the good weapons, shield and helmet the Princess provided for Sam – ' and he indicated the bundle on the floor – 'for this utility trash once authorized by the Camelot Armour and Weapons Board. *He-ha!*'

'Marvellous, darling!' said Ninette, as they began to exchange the ironmongery.

'Oh – just one of the amusing little ideas I've had, my dear Ninette. Let's put this stuff over there, then throw something over it – too heavy to cart around.'

'What I adore about helping you,' said Ninette with enthusiasm, 'is that you never stop having these brilliant original ideas, so there's lovely wicked plotting all the time, which is exactly what I've always wanted. Anything else, darling?'

'Yes,' said Malgrim. 'Stay behind and persuade him he needs a tankard of special Tournament Ale to give him courage.'

Ninette was delighted. 'And then you'll send him some abominable potion?'

'It'll render him faint and dizzy,' said Malgrim as he went. '*Ha-ha!*'

Ninette found a stool, brought it close to Sam's, arranged herself demurely on it, and that is how Sam found her when he came back, looking gloomier than ever.

'Oh – Sam – why so downcast?'

'Lamison said that Melicent wanted to speak to me,' said Sam. 'But I couldn't even get into the Royal Box – not properly dressed. Lamison must have been lying.'

'I've never thought him very truthful, Sam. Now wouldn't you like me to help you with your armour?'

'I'd like somebody to give me a hand, but not you.'

'Sam dear, you don't trust me?'

'No, Ninette dear. I'm a chump but not that much of a chump.'

'Oh – you are unfair. I've a good mind not to tell you about the special Tournament Ale.'

'Tournament Ale?' There was at last a faint hopefulness in Sam's voice.

'Brewed specially for competitors in tournaments. But of course it's no use my offering to bring you some.'

'Quite right.'

'But perhaps if I ask the barmaid to bring you some – '

'Barmaid? There isn't a barmaid here.'

'Of course there is,' said Ninette as she walked away. 'I'll send her along.'

Left to himself, Sam began looking at his armour and weapons. He gave the helmet a casual kick, and, to his astonishment and disgust, made a dent in it. He was about to try the sword when another unconscious bleeding knight was carried through the pavilion. Then when he did try the sword, bending it, instead of springing back it stayed bent. In despair he leant on the spear and immediately heard a crackling sound. He jumped forward, landing on the breastplate and apparently nearly splitting it. He limped back to his stool, cursing the whole idiotic business.

He was still sitting with his head in his hands when the barmaid from the Black Horse came in, carrying a pewter tankard.

'One Tournament Ale,' she announced in her usual toneless style.

'Thanks,' said Sam, taking it. 'Oh – it's you.'

'That's right. Turned out nice again.'

'I wish it hadn't. Well, I need this.' He emptied the tankard in one long go. 'Strong stuff. Bottle or barrel?'

'Don't ask me, Mr Penty. That chap with a black beard – illusionist – give it to me for you.'

'Malgrim?' Sam stared at her aghast.

'That's him. What's up? All right, isn't it?'

'I don't know yet,' said Sam uneasily. 'By the way, you haven't seen Captain Plunket – the Old Skipper, y'know, the chap who ordered all the double scotches?'

'No. Is *he* here?'

'He *was*.'

'I saw Mr Sanderson,' said the barmaid confidentially. 'He's offerin' ten to one on the Red Knight. They say he's murder, that Red Knight.'

Jack, the soldier, now looked in from the ground entrance. 'Get ready, chum. You're on next.'

Sam groaned as Jack's grinning face vanished. 'Help me on with this armour, please.'

She stared at him. 'You're not goin' out there, are you?'

'I have to.'

'My Gawd! Well, I don't know which goes where, but I'll do my best. An' you'll need all this an' more.' As she helped him with his buckling and fastening, she went on, 'Not very thick an' 'eavy, is it? Proper tinny stuff, I'd say. They ought to do better for you than this, if you ask me. You a visitor as well, not one of the regulars. I thought this armour'ud weigh tons.'

'It did when I first brought it here.'

'Perhaps somebody's changed it. 'Ow you feelin'?'

'Terrible.'

'You don't look a good colour. I wouldn't stay out long if I was you.'

'I don't expect to. Haven't got a couple of aspirins, have you?'

'Sorry, I'm right out of 'em.' She regarded him sympathetically, and made a clucking noise. 'Why don't you 'ave a nice lie down instead?'

'I'll be having one soon.'

Jack looked through the flap again. 'Which d'you fancy, chum – mounted or on foot?'

'On foot,' said Sam gloomily.

'Quite right. 'Aven't so far to fall. A minute to go, chum, then you're on. An' what a hope you've got!'

Sam tried moving around with his armour on and flourishing the sword, which was still bent.

'I've seen all this on the pickshers,' said the barmaid. 'But I don't fancy it somehow. Rather 'ave cowboys an' Indians. Or them gangsters in night-clubs. 'Course this is more *spectacular* – if that's what you fancy.'

'It's not what I fancy.' Sam was trying to straighten the sword.

A tremendous loud voice came through the flap. 'SIR SAM.'

'Coming,' Sam called miserably.

'Well, you've got a knight'ood out of it, 'aven't you? Best

of luck, dearie, an' just remember – there'll always be a Ningland.'

'Thanks very much,' said Sam. He tried to brace himself up, hurt something and groaned, then made his way out, to be greeted with a mixed outburst of cheering, booing, laughter. The barmaid, peeping through the flap, heard somebody behind her. It was Princess Melicent, who had come hurrying in, and she was extremely agitated.

'Tell me, have they begun? I thought I wouldn't mind, but now I daren't look. You'll have to tell me. What's happening?'

The barmaid looked. 'They're sort of walkin' round each other, dear. Oo – that Red Knight's a size, isn't he? Make two of poor Sir Sam. One-sided I call it. Oo – now they've started. Oh dear!'

Melicent, who could hear the sound of weapons clashing against armour, said hurriedly, 'Master Marlagram promised me it wouldn't be a real mortal combat. He said he'd work an enchantment somehow.'

'He'll 'ave to 'urry up then,' said the barmaid at her peephole.

'Who's winning?'

'Who d'you think, dear? Our chap 'asn't an earthly. Ref ought to stop it. Red Knight's beatin' 'im back – beatin' 'im back. Oo – what a slasher!'

'Oh – I can't bear it. I must find Marlagram.'

Even the barmaid was excited now. 'They're comin' this way – they're comin' this way. Sam's slipped. No, he's up again. Red Knight's at 'im again. They're comin' nearer an' nearer –'

Melicent ran towards the opposite entrance, shouting, 'Master Marlagram, where are you? Master Marlagram!' And she went out, still shouting.

As the clashing came nearer, the barmaid backed away from the entrance. Sam arrived first, backing in step by step, and trying desperately to ward off gigantic blows from the

Red Knight, who followed him in, an enormous ferocious figure in red armour and with red hair and beard sprouting from his helmet. But as soon as he was completely inside and had noticed the barmaid, the Red Knight stopped fighting at once.

'Two Tournament Ales,' he said.

'Two Tournament Ales – yes, sir,' said the barmaid, and trotted off down the pavilion.

The soldiers, Jack and Fred, were looking in, but the Red Knight jumped towards them, waving his sword. 'Keep out,' he roared. 'Keep out – ye misbegotten whoreson knaves – or I'll make sausages of your lights and livers.' Then he fastened the flap securely, sat on the nearest stool, loosened his upper armour and – to Sam's amazement – took off not only his helmet but the head that had been wearing it. Out of the

shirt below, like a sun rising, came the face of Captain Plunket, the Old Skip.

'Sit down, old boy,' said Plunket. 'But we'll have to keep
on making a clatter – or they'll wonder what's happening. So
just bash away at the nearest bit of armour. Like this.' And
he bashed away.

Sam was still recovering from the surprise. 'But, Skipper,
how do *you* come to be the Red Knight?'

'Enchantment, old boy. That fella Malgrim did it, last night.
Very thorough job too. I really felt I *was* the Red Knight –
ready to knock hell out of anybody – until a few minutes ago.
Then something happened – either more enchantment or
less. Believe it or not, that head I've just taken off was mine
until we got in here. Then I knew I could take it off. Back to
the Old Skipper again – and about time too.'

'But how am I going to kill you?' Sam was still feeling
dazed.

'Oh – we can work it. That's where the head comes in, I
fancy. Leave it to me, old boy. But keep the clatter going.'

'Trouble is, I must have been doped or something. I feel
dizzy.'

'Thought you weren't looking too good, Sam old boy.
Ever been doped on the Gold Coast? I was, one time. Didn't
come out of it for three weeks – and for two of 'em I thought
a dam' great spider was biting my toes. Witch-doctor stuff,
of course. Just as good as these fellas. Ah – here you are, my
dear.'

'Turned out nice again,' said the barmaid as she arrived
with two tankards.

'Thank you, dear.'

'None for me,' said Sam.

'Put the other down there then, dear,' said Plunket. 'Unless
you'd like it.'

'No, ta.' She looked very prim now. 'Never touch a drop
except for a gin an' pep if me tummy's a bit off.'

'Best thing for that,' Plunket told her, 'is a Valparaiso Mañana. Three of them – and you could eat a horse. And ten to one it's what you get too. Well – down the hatch!'

''Appy days!' She watched the Old Skipper empty his tankard. 'An' I'd rather keep you a week than a fortnight.'

Plunket ignored that remark. 'Now, dear, you'll have to give us a hand. Sam's groggy. Try and keep going a minute or two, Sam old boy. You help me with this armour, that's a good girl.' As they both set to work, he went on, 'We'll have to keep going somehow. Steady now for some Red Knight stuff.' And in a huge Red Knight voice, he bellowed, 'Surrender, you knock-kneed manikin! Surrender!'

Sam did his best. 'Never, never!'

'Louder. They'll never hear you, old boy.' Again, as the Red Knight, he roared, 'Surrender, I say.'

Sam produced something like a shout. 'Never!' Then he groaned: 'Crikey – that's given me a headache.'

'Now look, dear,' said Plunket, 'just keep clattering away with this sword while I take a breather and work something out.' Now out of his armour, with a tankard in each hand, he went closer to the entrance and shouted in his Red Knight voice, 'Nobody'll come in here – or else I'll slice his nose off.'

Sam, recovering a little, asked about Dimmock. 'What happened to him, Skip?'

'No idea, old boy. Malgrim turned me into the Red Knight before he started on Dimmock.' He looked at the barmaid, who was conscientiously banging away with the sword on the breastplate. 'Not getting tired, dear, are you?'

'A bit. But it makes a nice change.' She looked around as a *he-he-he!* came from somewhere. 'That's that very old conjurer. Get on your nerves, don't they?'

'Now, Sam old boy, can you pull yourself together just for half a minute?'

Sam got up, slowly and shakily. 'I'll try. What do I do?'

'Get ready to show 'em the head. When they've seen it, you be ready to run off with it, Violet.'

'Queenie.'

'Of course, Queenie. Well, Queenie dear, you run off with the head.'

'Where to?'

'Oh – anywhere. Ladies' cloakroom.'

'They won't want it in there.'

'Don't argue, Queenie dear. We haven't time. Now, Sam old boy, here's the sword and the head. Get ready to wave the sword and hold up the head when I open that entrance. Stand clear for the Red Knight's death scene.' He took his own sword from the barmaid, banged hard with it, then roared in his Red Knight voice, 'Mercy! Have mercy, Sir Sam! O-o-o-oh!' He threw down the sword. 'Now, here we go, chaps.' He rushed the barmaid towards the entrance, unfastened the flap and shouted, 'He's done it. He's done it.'

'Sam's won,' the barmaid screeched. 'Sam's won.'

Sam waved the sword and held up the head as the cheering crowd rushed in. Plunket supported Sam and then tossed the head to the barmaid, who ran off with it as if she were playing at Twickenham.

'Sir Sam's all right,' Plunket announced. 'Not badly hurt. But give him air – give him air.'

Melicent was there now. 'Oh – Sam darling,' she cried, embracing him, 'it was wonderful. You're not hurt, are you?'

'No, darling,' he replied with an effort, 'just dizzy – that's all.'

'Stout fella,' said King Meliot. 'Well, you can take it easy now – for an hour or so. The dragon's in position down in the wood, but it's asleep. Better not wake it up yet.'

Sam gave a gasp and slithered down to his knees, almost out.

'Must knight you properly too,' said the King, not a perceptive man. He touched Sam on the shoulder with his sword, and this sent Sam further down. 'Arise, Sir Sam.' But Sam was out cold. 'We said – *Arise, Sir Sam.*'

'Oh, Father, don't be idiotic,' cried Melicent, kneeling beside Sam. 'Help me with him – you men.'

Four men, under the direction of Melicent, carried Sam out of the pavilion. King Meliot, Captain Plunket, and various top Peradore people, afraid of missing something, followed Sir Sam and the Princess, but the crowd remained behind.

'Well, people,' Mr Sanderson shouted, 'the favourite's lost – an' I'm paying out ten to one on Sir Sam. Anybody lucky?'

'Yes, me, Mr Sanderson,' said the barmaid, emerging with her betting slip.

'That's right, Queenie, you're the lucky lady today.' He handed her a bag of money. 'Now, friends – here's your chance to get your money back. I'm offerin' eleven to two on the dragon – eleven to two against Sir Sam. Here's another chance to back your boy, the chance you missed before. Eleven to two on the dragon.' And business was brisk.

CHAPTER THIRTEEN

Dragon Lore

Sam, resting in a small tent just behind the Royal Stand, had just finished toying with a second breakfast when Melicent arrived with her father. She was carrying a tattered cloak and an almost equally tattered old manuscript volume.

'How are you feeling now, Sir Sam?' asked the King.

'Better than I did, Your Majesty. Though not too bright.'

'Dragon's still asleep, but it'll be waking soon. So, if you're taking it on, you'd better get ready, my boy.'

'But, Father,' Melicent protested, 'you have to explain first. You promised, don't forget.'

'So we did. Well, this is the situation, my dear fella. You're now Sir Sam – conqueror of the Red Knight – and of course no more dungeon for you. You're free. Give you a note to King Arthur if you like. Might get you high priority for a quest, or a special damsel-rescuing expedition.'

'He's not going on any damsel-rescuing expedition,' said Melicent. 'I know those damsels.'

'Thank you, sire,' said Sam. 'But I'd rather stay here in Peradore. What about this dragon?'

'We're coming to that,' said the King. 'Now you have the choice. You're free to go. No dragon, if you don't want to take it on. But no dragon, no daughter. Can't marry Melicent if you don't fight the dragon.'

'You have to choose, Sam,' said Melicent anxiously.

'I see,' said Sam thoughtfully. 'What – er – sort of dragon is this? Just a little one, perhaps?'

'Not at all.' King Meliot spoke with unnecessary enthusiasm. 'First-class dragon. Only caught a glimpse of it, but seemed a magnificent brute. And fiery of course – the real thing. Even sound asleep it was sending up a lot of smoke. You couldn't want a better dragon.'

'I don't,' said Sam unhappily. 'You do realize, Melicent my love, I don't know how to fight a dragon. Never even seen one before.'

'Yes, Sam.' She regarded him gravely. 'You'll have to be very very brave. And perhaps I'm not worth it.'

'You don't believe that, do you?'

'Frankly, no, darling. Any girl who did wouldn't be worth marrying.'

'All right. I'll have a bash at it.'

'Oh – Sam!'

'Good man,' said King Meliot. 'By the way, it's a private contest this time. No spectators allowed.'

'I'm glad to hear it.'

'That's the rule now. Last time the public were admitted, about fifty of 'em got hurt. When a big dragon, like this one, really gets desperate – '

'No, please, Father,' cried Melicent.

'In the stories I used to read,' said Sam wistfully, 'the dragon-challenger usually had some magic help – an invisible cloak – '

'Well, there's this cloak.' Melicent held up the gaudy but sadly tattered thing she had brought. She spread it out to show the holes. 'It's awfully moth-eaten – look. And of course where the holes are, you won't be invisible. But at least it might *confuse* the dragon.'

'Better than nothing,' said Sam hopefully. 'Some of me would be invisible.'

Melicent exchanged a glance with her father. 'I'm afraid there's another difficulty, Sam darling. Father, you tell him.'

'Fact is, my boy, we're not certain about this cloak,' said the King cheerfully. 'Haven't had it out for years. Now it's a dragon-challenger's cloak, no doubt about that. But there are two kinds, and we can't remember which this is. There's the cloak that makes you invisible to the dragon. But there's also the dragon-arousing cloak specially designed and coloured to make the dragon very angry and full of fight.'

'And you can't remember which this is?' Sam was indignant.

'I'm afraid not, darling,' said Melicent. 'Isn't it a nuisance? Of course the holes might make him less angry – '

'The cloak's out,' said Sam firmly. 'No cloak. Haven't you anything else?'

She showed him the ancient manuscript volume she had also brought. 'Well, there are these old instructions about how to deal with the different kinds of dragons. I'm afraid they're not easy to follow.'

'Have to puzzle it out between you,' said the King. 'Your eyes are younger than ours.'

Melicent now sat beside Sam, with the volume between them. 'Now we know this is a fiery dragon – '

'*And* big,' said Sam gloomily. 'Turn to the larger sizes.'

Melicent whipped over several pages. 'It says here that if the beast be shovel-tailed, then you must crouch low and to the left when it makes its first spring. Do you think you can remember that, darling?'

'I doubt it. And *is* this one shovel-tailed? And what happens if it isn't?'

Melicent read on. 'It says if it's a narrow-tailed dragon with a yellow cross underneath, you mustn't crouch low but jump high to the right.'

'I dare say,' said Sam crossly. 'But I can't ask the thing if it's got a yellow cross underneath. And what if I jump high to the right when I ought to have crouched low to the left? Curtains.'

'But if it's a horny short-tail, this man says, you must simply keep moving all the time.'

'Yes, yes. But how the blazes do I know if it's a horny short-tail or a yellow-cross narrow-tail or a shovel-tail? I thought there were just dragons – a standard line – but not all these varieties.'

'Only saw it a long way off,' said King Meliot. 'But it looked like a shovel-tail to us. Better not count on it, though.'

'What do I count on?'

'Use your own judgement, my boy. Oh – before we forget – our chief armourer has a special sword for you. Two-handed, of course. Ordinary sword won't make any impression on a dragon of that size. Well now – best of luck, Sir Sam. And remember, if you do decide it's a shovel-tail, then crouch low and to the left for its first spring.'

'Thank you, sire. But I think I'll try the horny-short-tail technique and keep moving all the time. But leave the instruction book.'

'Oh – Sam – I'm beginning to feel frightened now,' said Melicent.

'So am I. Just listen to this: *If the beast should have a broad fishtail with scarlet markings, then at the first pounce it be best to spring high into the air. But there's a snag. Yet divers of these broad fishtail dragons have a foul trick of swinging upward with their monstrous forepaws* – Oh, murder!'

King Meliot, who had left the tent, was making impatient noises outside. Melicent gave Sam a hasty kiss. 'I've been trying to find Master Marlagram, darling, but he seems to have disappeared.'

'Try again, sweetheart. Don't stop trying,' Sam said urgently. 'If ever an enchanter was needed, it's now.'

When she had gone, Sam closed his eyes, vainly attempting to relax. Was it a shovel-tail, a narrow-tail, a horny short-tail, a broad fishtail? Or were there half a dozen other kinds, waiting for him in the later pages of this cursed book? He opened his eyes, to see the chief armourer holding out a sword as big as himself.

'A lovely job,' said the chief armourer. 'Got the weight, but keen-edged too. You could cut a hair in two with this sword.'

'But I don't want to cut a hair in two – worse luck,' Sam told him. 'The point is – will it cut a dragon in two?'

'Well,' said the chief armourer slowly, 'yes and no. It will if you've got a shovel-tail or a narrow-tail. But if you've got a horny short-tail or a broad fishtail – '

'Oh, shut up,' said Sam in disgust.

'Then again,' the chief armourer continued, 'take your wedge-tail or your big fiery curly-tail – '

But Sam put his hands to his ears.

CHAPTER FOURTEEN

Operation Dragon

You have only to imagine a beautiful glade in high summer – then this is the one. In the centre of it, at ease on a mossy rock, was Captain Plunket. He was smoking a cheroot and keeping an eye on the dragon. Its enormous head could just be seen between a sycamore and an oak. It was still asleep; its eyes were closed; and puffs of smoke were coming regularly out of its nostrils.

A narrow path entered the glade at a right angle to where the dragon was lying. Along this path, looking rather bedraggled and weary, came Anne Dutton-Swift and Peggy, the secretary. Seeing them, Plunket pushed himself up from his rock, and smiled.

'Good morning,' said Anne Dutton-Swift.

'Good morning, ladies.'

'We must look a sight. We've had a dreadful time. Wandered about all yesterday afternoon and evening, though we could see the castle in the distance – '

'We ought to have turned to the left, like I said,' Peggy told her.

'Spent the night in a barn, then got lost in this wood.' Anne looked with some curiosity at Plunket's costume, a mixture of the modern and the medieval. 'Tell me, are you one of us or one of them?'

'Depends who you are, doesn't it?' said Plunket.

'I'm Anne Dutton-Swift – of Wallaby, Dimmock, Paly and Tooks, the advertising agency.'

'And I'm Peggy, Mr Dimmock's secretary.'

'Then I'm one of you. Cap'n Plunket, ladies – the Old Skipper.'

'Why, of course,' cried Anne, delighted. 'You're the heavenly man who did the film about the fish that could climb trees.'

Equally delighted, Plunket insisted upon shaking hands with her. 'Knew I'd meet somebody one day who'd seen that film. And now here you are. Good-lookin' woman too. Wonderful.'

'Yes, isn't it? Just gorgeous meeting you here of all places. Always longed to tell you how much I liked that film. Did it really climb a tree?'

'Well, it did and it didn't. Tell you all about it later.'

Peggy, who had been listening with some impatience to this exchange of compliments, now broke in, severely, 'Mr Dimmock *is* here, isn't he?'

'He *was*,' said Plunket. 'Last night we had a few flagons and stoups together, but then we ran into trouble and now he seems to have disappeared. Enchantment probably.'

'How marvellous!' Anne cried. 'Is there really enchantment here?'

'Place is stiff with it,' Plunket told her. 'Early this morning, I was a huge Red Knight – about seven foot high with ginger hair bristling all over my face. Felt like him too for a time. Knocked everybody for six at the tournament. As for Dimmock, I'll try to find out what's happened to him – once this dragon business is settled.'

'Oh – there's dragon business, is there?' said Peggy suspiciously. 'Where?'

'Here. I was just having a quiet smoke with the dragon. Look – there he is.' He pointed.

'Oh – my goodness!' Anne was alarmed. 'And I thought they never existed.'

'They do here. Different set-up altogether. But don't worry about this dragon. He's still asleep – and probably won't wake up until Sam's ready to challenge him.'

'Sam Penty?'

'Yes. Sir Sam now, by the way.'

'Oh – Sam's in this, is he?' said Peggy bitterly. 'He would be. Typical artist. We have more trouble with them than with all the rest combined. He ought to be hard at work for Wallaby, Dimmock, Paly and Tooks now, not challenging dragons. His holiday isn't till September.'

'Captain Plunket,' said Anne appealingly, 'do take pity on us, and tell us what we ought to do visitor-wise. The castle, do you think?'

'Certainly. I'll show you the way.' He brought them to another path. 'Straight along here, then take the first turn to the left – and you can't miss it. Sorry I can't come with you, but I have to keep an eye on this dragon, for Sam.'

'Thank you *so* much,' said Anne, smiling at him. And then when they were a few yards along the path, she said to Peggy in a loud clear voice, 'I think he's a sweet man, don't you?'

'No,' said Peggy.

Plunket returned to his rock, relit his cheroot and puffed away with the dragon. Several minutes later, Sam arrived, already looking weary, with the ancient dragon volume under one arm and the enormous sword trailing behind him.

'Hello, Skip! I'm just about all-in. Where's the dragon?'

'Over there, old boy. See him? Still sound asleep. Must have had a dam' good breakfast off somebody. Not feeling too good?'

'No. What – er – sort of dragon is it?'

'I won't deceive you, old boy. He's big – a socking great brute. And he's got everything but the kitchen stove. Look.'

Sam looked. 'He's got the kitchen stove too,' he said gloomily. He sat down and opened the ancient volume.

'No time for reading – surely, old boy?'

'It's a dragon-fighters' instruction book the King dug out for me,' said Sam, still turning the pages. 'I dunno – the old man really is a bit slap-happy.'

'Only king I knew really well was Um-dunga-sloo, way

back, of the Ivory Coast. Sold him two hundred and fifty alarm clocks and five gramophones. Only one of 'em worked.'

'Let's stick to the dragon.' Sam was worried. 'Now would you say it's a shovel-tail, a narrow-tail with a yellow cross, a horny short-tail, or a broad short-tail with scarlet markings?'

'Haven't a clue, old boy. And you can please yourself, but I don't propose to go and examine his tail.'

'Neither do I,' said Sam, dipping into the instruction book again.

Plunket stared at the dragon. The puffs of smoke from its nostrils were larger and coming out faster. 'I think he's getting steam up.'

'Oh – lord!' Sam looked up in despair.

Plunket shook hands with him. 'Well, all the best, old boy. Like to give you a hand, but of course it's against the rules. But I won't be far. Just along this path. Good luck, old boy.'

Making sure that the dragon was not watching him, Sam tried a swing or two with the two-handed sword, finding it appallingly hard to manage. A lot of smoke was coming from the dragon now, and great snorting and puffing noises, like an angry train. Sam went closer, to take a look at it, then retreated again.

'*Pst.*' This was Plunket, who had returned to the edge of the glade. 'Anything happening?' he enquired in a loud whisper.

'Not yet. But he sounds as big as a railway train.'

'Have to challenge him, y'know, old boy. One of the rules.'

'I wish you'd shut up about the rules.'

'Take it easy, Sam old boy. Leave you to it now, eh?'

'Yes. This challenging's going to sound ridiculous.' He braced himself, grasped the sword firmly, and went fairly close to the dragon. 'Look here,' he began in a loud but uneasy voice, 'I'm challenging you to – er – combat. But we needn't make it mortal – what d'you think?'

The dragon opened an eye, yellowish and about the size of a soup plate. Sam stepped back a pace or two.

'Well, what d'you think? Why not a few friendly rounds – and leave it at that? The exercise'll do you good. You're smoking too much. But of course I'm challenging you. Don't make any mistake about that.'

'Sam,' said the dragon, 'stop it.'

'Stop it?' Sam was astonished.

'Yes, it's only me.'

'How d'you mean it's only you?'

'It's *me* – Dimmock.'

'Dimmock? What are you doing inside the dragon?'

'I'm not *inside* the dragon,' said Dimmock crossly. 'I *am* the dragon.'

'How do you know you're Dimmock then?'

'Because I do. How do you know you're Sam Penty? And don't think I enjoy being a dragon. It's like having an acid stomach ten feet long.' He coughed. 'So hot and smoky too.'

'How did it happen?'

'That enchanter, Malgrim, did it. After he turned the Skipper into the Red Knight, he turned me into a dragon.'

'But look here,' said Sam, 'I'm supposed to knock you off in order to marry Melicent.'

'Now don't be silly, Sam,' said Dimmock hastily. 'You and I have always been good friends. None of the firm's artists has been treated better than you. If you feel you ought to have a rise, I'll gladly take it up with the board –'

'Wait a minute,' said Sam. 'To begin with, I don't intend to go back to the job. And you couldn't take anything up with the board, looking like that, could you? The point is – what am I going to do? I promised to challenge the dragon –'

'Yes, but not *me*. Go and find a proper dragon.'

'No, you're the dragon I'm supposed to overcome. Nothing said about any other dragon.'

'Yes, Sam. But if you have me disenchanted – or whatever they call it here – and then I'm me again and there's no dragon, then that's the same thing. So you go and find

that enchanter. Or the other one – the old one. If necessary,
I'm prepared to offer one of them a seat on the board. Put it
in writing too. Peggy's here, isn't she? Thought I heard her
voice.' He opened his enormous dragon mouth, to call her.
'Peggy. Peggy.'

Somebody came running at full speed through the wood.
Of course it was Peggy, notebook in hand. When she arrived,
she showed no surprise, leaving it all to Sam. 'Yes, Mr Dimmock?'

'Take a letter to Mr Paly. *Dear Herbert – I'm writing this from
a place called Peradore, where I ran into a little trouble –* He broke
off, as he saw that Sam had not moved and that Plunket was
now approaching. 'Don't just stand there staring at us, Sam – '

'If you saw a dragon dictating letters to a secretary, you'd
want to stare,' Sam told him.

'Go and find those enchanters. It's just as important for
you as it is for me. Skipper, you go with him.'

'Dimmock, is it?' said Plunket. 'Tell me, old boy, do you
feel like a dragon?'

'I did – very nasty too – but it's worn off. Now, Skipper,
you go with Sam and get me disenchanted.'

'Can do, old boy. But in the meantime we can't have you
staying here, dictating letters. You're supposed to have been
rubbed out by Sam. You'll have to hide in the wood while
you're still a dragon.'

'All right. But hurry up with it.'

'By the way,' said Sam, 'this could be important for the
record. Do you happen to know what kind of dragon you
are? I mean, are you a shovel-tail, a narrow-tail – '

'I'm a big fiery curly-tail,' said Dimmock, not without a
touch of pride.

'I'll have to look them up,' said Sam. 'Well, we'll do what
we can, but for Pete's sake don't lie there the rest of the
morning, dictating letters. Come on, Skipper.'

'That's right, off you go. Now – where was I, Peggy?'

'*Ran into a little trouble,*' Peggy repeated.

'Full stop there. Next: *But with a bit of luck everything now might work out for the best. There are some enchanters here, and one of them might like to come on to the board. This means, as we have often agreed, dropping old Wallaby, but also, the way I see it, getting rid of Tooks* – Now what d'you want?' He was glaring at Sam and Plunket, who were back again.

'Don't look like that, old boy,' said Plunket. 'You're forgetting you've got eyes like headlamps.'

'I'm trying to finish this letter. What do you fellows want?'

'It's this sword, Dimmock,' said Sam apologetically. 'I'm supposed to have killed you with it – and look at it. Ought to be dripping with dragon's blood. And ten to one it's a special sort of blood that old Meliot would recognize at a glance.'

'Absolutely,' said Plunket. 'So we need a little co-operation here, old boy. Just a thrust or two somewhere – '

It may have been Dimmock protesting but the noise was a real dragon noise, and they must have heard it up in the castle, where they probably imagined the beast was in its death throes.

'Play the game, Dimmock old boy,' said Plunket reproachfully. 'And don't let go like that again. Terrible reek of sulphur.'

'Just make it a scratch somewhere then,' said Dimmock.

'Not possible,' said Sam. 'Take a look at yourself. It would be like trying to scratch a socking great tank. Has to be a deep thrust.'

'Here, give me that sword,' said Dimmock impatiently. One of his vast claws lifted it to his mouth, and then he chewed off most of the blade, and dropped the hilt and the little that remained of the blade at Sam's feet. 'If that doesn't convince 'em, nothing will.'

'I must say, old boy,' said Plunket, 'I'm thankful you *are* Dimmock. Now we know the form, there's one man doesn't take on any dragons here – and that's the Old Skip.'

'Oh – go away. Where was I, Peggy? Oh – yes – Tooks.

*With the set-up I have in mind, Herbert, Tooks would never fit in
– too narrow-minded and has not got the enterprise. We might try
one of the enchanters looking after finance and the firm's taxation
problems –*

'A keen type,' said Plunket to Sam as they left the glade,
'but he oughtn't to overdo it. Ought to relax more. By the
way, old boy, tell me about this Anne Dutton-Swift.'

CHAPTER FIFTEEN

All a Bit Much

'The truth is,' said Anne Dutton-Swift to Plunket, 'that I'm not hep, as the boys say, enchanter-wise. Explain, please, Skip.'

'Like lightning, my dear. Malgrim rushed back here, found that Dimmock and I had been put under arrest by King Meliot, and asked if he could go to work on us – '

'Enchanter-wise?'

'Enchanter-wise. He turned me into this Red Knight, Dimmock into a dragon. And, let's face it, he did a nice job. But old Marlagram, who looks past it but isn't, then came tearing back, *he-he-he*-ing like mad, and trumped Malgrim's ace.'

'Not bridge, Skip darling. I hate bridge.'

'So do I,' said Plunket. 'Poker or nothing, I say. Did I ever tell you – no, some other time. But old Marlagram prophesied that Peradore would be threatened by a terrible Red Knight and a dragon, and the King agreed that whoever overcame them should marry his daughter. This really meant it was all in the bag for Sam.'

'Hence – and I never remember using that word before – this betrothal ceremony. Sam looks rather sweet, doesn't he?'

'Well, the King, who's a bit of a stickler, can't say he's improperly dressed – Peradore-wise.'

Sam, standing in front of the King and waiting now to be joined by Melicent, was wearing a short cloak, doublet and hose. His right leg was apple-green, his left was striped green-and-white, his doublet was a pale pink, and his cloak a darker green. 'If his thighs were bigger,' said Plunket, 'he'd look like a Principal Boy in a pantomime. I must tell you – no, not now, it'll keep.'

'I wonder what Melicent will be wearing.' Miss Dutton-Swift sounded wistful.

'Whatever it is, it's keeping her too long. Old Meliot's getting impatient. Look at him. He'll blow up in a minute, and somebody will be put under arrest.'

'I don't see either of the enchanters,' said Anne, looking round the crowded banqueting hall.

'Busy elsewhere, I'll bet. Now then – what's happening?'

The chief herald, misinterpreting an impatient glance from the King, now began: 'Hear ye! Hear ye! Hear ye! His Royal Majesty, King Meliot of Peradore – High Lord of Bergamore, Marralore and Parlot – '

'No, no, no,' the King bellowed. 'Can't start yet. Where's our daughter? Where *is* that confounded girl? Bring her down, somebody. Don't care if she hasn't finished dressing. We can't wait any longer.'

Sam, who had been feeling anxious for some time, noticed that Ninette was not among the ladies-in-waiting, who now picked up their skirts and went tripping off to fetch Melicent. No Ninette, and no Malgrim? Were they up to something? Marlagram would know, but he was missing too.

'Torches, torches,' the King commanded. It was late, and there was little daylight left.

The ladies-in-waiting returned, fluttering and shrieking, 'Your Majesty, Your Majesty, Princess Melicent isn't there. She's vanished.'

'Vanished? Nonsense! Search the castle. Look everywhere.' King Meliot turned to his counsellors. 'Just like her mother. First, she wanted to marry this fella, and then, when we give our consent, she refuses to attend the betrothal ceremony. All the same.'

'I have often thought, sire,' the oldest counsellor began ponderously, 'that women – '

'So have we, so have we,' cried the King. 'Now then – find her, find her – search everywhere. Isn't there an enchanter here? If you can't find our daughter, find an enchanter.'

Sam made his way to where Plunket and Anne Dutton-Swift were standing. 'Have you seen old Marlagram? No? Then we're sunk, if you ask me. Ten to one, Malgrim and Ninette are at it again. Marlagram,' he called, 'where are you? What's become of Melicent? How do I find her?'

'Go down to the darkest corner of the dungeon.' The voice, small but clear, seemed to come from some great distance.

'Is that you, Marlagram?'

'*He-he-he!*'

'That's undoubtedly the old boy, old boy,' said Plunket. 'Better try the dungeon.'

'But don't spoil those lovely clothes, Sam,' said Anne.

'Blow the clothes! I must get a torch. See you later.'

Torch in hand, Sam pushed past all the people milling around, ran down a lot of steps, and was out of breath by the time he reached the dungeon. Making his way into the darkest corner, he forgot how slippery the floor was there, fell on his back, his legs in the air, and slid forward. A wind came roaring. There were lights, noises, a lot of people. He scrambled to his feet in his own never-had-it-so-good world. Two girls were giving him a hand.

'This is just the shade I was telling you about, Edna,' one of them was saying. 'This green – look. Ever so nice.'

'Where am I?' Sam asked them. 'What *is* this?'

'Go on, who you kidding? Dressed like this too.'

'He must be with Frozen Marrowfats,' said Edna. 'They've a castle – all Middle Ages style – remember?'

'Look – I'm not kidding. Must have lost my memory when I fell. Where is this and what's happening? Looks like Olympia.'

'I'll buy it,' said Edna. 'If you've really forgotten, this is the Canned and Frozen Foods Exhibition of 1961.'

'Thanks very much,' said Sam. 'Well, I must look for my girl-friend. She must be here or I wouldn't be here. So long.'

Much to his relief, his costume did not attract much attention, just a few smiles from the women and grins from the men. He lingered at a stall where a buxom woman was demonstrating Mrs Friendly's Instant Scrambled Eggs. Just when the scrambled eggs, smoking hot, were turned out on to a plate, the six people who had been watching her began to move away. The buxom woman looked at their backs with disgust. 'I don't know how you're finding 'em here,' she said to Sam, as one demonstrator to another. 'But as far as I'm concerned, they're the kiss of death. Everybody saying "Wait till we get to London!" Well, we're in London, aren't we? And give me Manchester and Birmingham. They're blarzy here, that's what's wrong with 'em – too blarzy. Couldn't do with a snack, dear, could you?'

'Yes, I could,' said Sam. 'I'm hungry.'

'Then do me a favour – eat this lot. Sales manager might pop along any minute, and it looks better if somebody's trying 'em.'

Sam accepted the fork she offered him, and then watched her shaking plenty of salt and pepper on the eggs. He must have looked dubious as she handed him the plate.

'Oh – they're not too bad. Ropy and on the musty side, but I've had worse – I think. If you need something to wash 'em down, I've a bottle of beer at the back, but you'll have to get it down quick.'

'Who's Mrs Friendly?'

'She's a factory in New Jersey, dear. And another one going up in Portland, Oregon. I'll make a dive for the beer.'

'I'm looking for my girl,' Sam explained, after he had dealt with the eggs and hastily swallowed the beer. 'Her name's Melicent. She's a blonde – a real one – and ravishingly pretty –'

'Isn't that nice?'

'She'll be dressed in the medieval style – like me. You haven't seen her, have you?'

'Haven't seen anybody you could call anybody tonight, dear.' She called to the woman opposite who was looking after somebody's canned custard, 'What's the matter with 'em tonight? Where are they all going? Oh – the Cake Mix Competition.' She turned to Sam. 'You'd better try the Cake Mix Competition. Along there somewhere, dear.'

Where the stalls ended, people were wedged in front of a curtained platform, with a loudspeaker on each side of it. Sam, at the back of the crowd and not yet free of the stalls, was only just able to get a glimpse of four girls, competitors perhaps, who were standing at one side of the platform, facing half a dozen persons sitting at ease and presumably acting as judges. There were some TV cameras turning, little jokes coming out of the loudspeakers like announcements of doomsday, and the kind of idiot applause that is a feature of all these functions. There was something vaguely familiar about the voice of the master of ceremonies. No, it couldn't be. Yes, but it was – Malgrim.

'I will now ask Lady Ninette,' he was saying, 'to announce the judges' decision. Lady Ninette.' More applause, of course.

Ninette might have been doing this sort of thing for years. She had just the right manner, the right accent. 'On-ah behalf-ah av thay panal av judges,' she proclaimed, 'Oi-ah dar wish to say-ah – we've all bin delaighted heah bay the estonaishin'lay haigh stendard av the competitahs this ev'naing – much plaishah to tell yo' we have unainimouslay decidaid that the winnah is Melicent Peradore.' More applause.

'Thank you, Lady Ninette,' cried Malgrim. 'So, by a unanimous decision of our judges, Melicent Peradore is Miss Nutty Cake Mix of 1961.' Cheers, applause, boos, and a fanfare from three trumpeters of the Guards. Half out of his mind, Sam could just see Melicent, dazed or dreamy, being pushed towards the microphone. 'Congratulations, Melicent, on being Miss Nutty Cake Mix of 1961! Now – what do you want?'

'You know what I want,' said Melicent. 'I want Sam.'

'I'm here,' Sam yelled, trying to plunge forward. But it was then that he fatally entangled himself with Ferguson's Frozen Fillets.

'What's the idea?' demanded the man in charge, a big tough type, probably off a trawler. 'Look at them fillets.'

'Get out of my way.' Sam gave him a shove. The next moment they were slugging it out, the stall was swaying, and it was raining frozen fillets. But just as he was thinking about a good left hook, Sam's arms were seized from behind, somebody gave him a fearful conk, and he was out. . . .

'Now you're feeling a bit better,' the inspector was saying, 'we'll start again. And this time we won't have any double talk about princesses and dragons. Your name?'

'Algrim,' said Sam. There was a cup of tea in front of him. It seemed to be cuppa time at the police station, everybody had one. 'M. Algrim.' He drank some tea.

'Full name, come along. M for what?'

'Maurice.'

'Maurice Algrim – living where?'

'10d Meliot Terrace, N.W. 9,' Sam replied promptly.

'Occupation?'

'I'm an electronic computer adjuster – very important. They

can make some bad mistakes even when they *are* adjusted, but when they aren't they go haywire.'

'And so do you, Mr Algrim,' said the inspector severely. He had a long thin face, and his eyes were so close to his nose that he looked like an enormous insect or somebody from another planet. 'A responsible man like you – what are you doing in those clothes and why did you cause a disturbance at the Exhibition?'

'It's a long story,' said Sam, desperately wondering what it would be, 'and I don't want to bore you.'

'I'll let you know when I'm losing interest.' The inspector looked round for appreciation, and two young constables choked over their tea.

'I'm dressed like this because I was taking the place of my cousin, who's with Frozen Marrowfats. They're wearing fancy costume this year. I'd gone along to look at the Nutty Cake Mix Competition because a girl I know was in it. I saw her on the platform and thought she looked ill. I tried to get nearer, having given her a shout to tell her I was there. You'd have done the same yourself, wouldn't you?'

'No,' said the inspector. 'But when does the fighting start?'

'I tried to push past that Ferguson's Frozen Fillets chap, and he was very truculent, asked me what the idea was, then we were mixing it, all among the frozen fillets. My arms were held – mine, not his – and somebody behind hit me with something, probably a frozen codfish – I can still feel it. And as far as I know, I'm the only one that got hurt.'

'As far as *you* know,' said the inspector very slowly. His tone suggested that at least six other persons, probably women and children, had died since the scuffle ended. 'But there might be some things you don't know, mightn't there, Mr Algrim? However, this time you happen to be right. And as no charge is being preferred and Ferguson's didn't call us in the first place and their chap says it might have been six of one and half a dozen of the other, I'm letting you go – but

don't get into any more trouble, especially with those tights
on. Good-night, Mr Algrim.'

Outside, Sam's late opponent, the trawler type, was standing in front of an enormous limousine. In it were two other
men, probably trawler types, and three large women, all of
them roaring and screaming with laughter over a midnight
picnic.

'Glad to see you're out of there, mate,' said Sam's man,
holding out his hand for Sam to shake. 'No hard feelings, eh?
That's the way – good old English style. If you'd had a knife,
I'd have felt different.'

'I'd have felt different if I could have landed that left hook,'
said Sam. 'But that's when they held my arms.'

'I saw it coming. I was ready for it. And I didn't ask 'em to
interfere, did I? Well, no harm's been done.'

'What about all those fillets?'

'Dummies. Shake again, mate. You're not going Grimsby
way, are you?'

'No, thanks. In fact, you're the first man I've ever met who
was going Grimsby way.'

'Must get on then. All the best, mate.'

Sam watched him join the red-faced picnic party, then
waited to see the limousine glide away. Without thinking
where he was going, he started walking. It was late now, well
after midnight, and not only was London already shuttered
and dark but it looked as if it might never open again. Light
rain, which might soon be heavy rain, was falling. Sam felt
miserable.

It was not long before he felt much worse. Stretching before him, going on and on until it reached either a pension and
Bournemouth or death, was the Cromwell Road. Then it was
that there came into Sam's aching head the terrible thought
that he had not come from Peradore to find Melicent, there
was no Melicent, no Peradore, he had dreamt it all, and was
probably suffering now from too long and thick a night at the

Black Horse or the Chelsea Arts Club. All that had happened, he began to feel, was that he had let his imagination play around that Damosel Stockings job too long. King Meliot and the two enchanters, the tournament in the sun and the dragon's glade in the green shadow, even Melicent herself, were all fading fast. Reality was this darkness, this rain, this mournful length of Cromwell Road. He could have wept.

A taxi came along. Wondering how much change he had, he tried to put a hand into his trousers pocket. But his hand slipped down the damp side of his hose. Doublet and hose, of course! What did that mean, then? It wasn't the first time he had worn fancy dress. Before he could puzzle this out, the taxi stopped.

'But you've got a fare,' said Sam, disappointed.

'She won't mind,' said the driver. '*He-he-he!*'

'Marlagram?'

'Oh – do get in, darling,' said Melicent. 'Goodness – you're wet.'

'But how – what – where – why – ?'

'Where to, sir?' said Marlagram, overdoing his taxi-driver act.

'Twice round the park,' said Sam happily, 'and then – Peradore.'

'What park?'

'Any park.'

It was in Regent's Park that the policeman stopped them. 'Let's see your licence,' he said to Marlagram.

'Certainly – *he-he-he!* But why see just one? Here's five hundred of 'em, lad. Ready for Peradore, you two love-birds?'

'At this point,' said the policeman, consulting his notes, to the sergeant later, 'after handing me this armful of stuff, the driver vanished, along with his two passengers, leaving me with the empty taxicab and no clue as to who'd been driving it or who'd been riding in it. An' that's the honest truth, Sarge, all as true as I'm here. Oh – there's just another thing.

I think he said they were all going to Peradore.'

'An' now I'll tell you where you're going to, if you're not careful, me lad,' the sergeant began. But why should we care, if we too can return to Peradore?

CHAPTER SIXTEEN

Business With Enchanters

It was luncheon-time in the cottage shared by Marlagram and Malgrim. Marlagram went into the tiny dining-room, sat down, and, as if addressing an invisible waiter, said, 'Bowl o' porridge – sharp.'

As soon as the bowl, a large one, appeared on the table, Marlagram began eating the porridge in rather a slobbering, disgusting fashion, spilling a lot of it on his beard. His nephew, Malgrim, who arrived a few minutes later, glanced with contempt at the messy old man before sitting down.

This did not worry Marlagram. 'Have a bowl o' porridge, lad, like me,' he said.

'Great Beelzebub – no.' Malgrim shuddered. 'I don't have to eat slops.' He fixed his gaze and concentrated his attention on the space above the table. 'Duck and green peas,' he told it sharply. 'And a flagon of Bordeaux.' Then he waited a couple of minutes, but nothing happened. 'Didn't you hear me? I want duck and green peas and a flagon of Bordeaux.'

'*He-he-he!*' Marlagram raised his spoon. 'Bowl o' porridge – sharp.'

The porridge arrived at once in front of Malgrim, who jumped up and said angrily, 'This is intolerable, Uncle. We agreed from the first that no matter what professional magical moves we might have to make against each other, neither of us would interfere with the domestic arrangements. You've broken our agreement.'

'Who started breaking agreements? You did, lad.'

'I wish you'd wipe that porridge off your beard.'

'Don't change the subject. When King Meliot arranged

that betrothal ceremony last night, you'd lost an' I'd won.
You thought you were a move ahead, lad – *he-he-he!* – rushing
back here to do your Red Knight and dragon transformations
– and all the time you were working for me an' didn't know
it. Right?'

'It was one of your smarter moves, I must admit,' said
Malgrim grudgingly. 'Obviously I underestimated you. But – '

'Hold on, lad, I haven't finished. Then, against all the rules,
you go an' muck up that betrothal ceremony by luring poor
Melicent out of real life. So, just when I thought I could ease
up a bit, I have to go an' work fast and hard. I even had to
pretend to be driving a horseless carriage, which is more than
you've ever had to do. You weren't playing the game, lad,
an' you know it. You're nearly as bad as one of Morgan le
Fay's sorceresses, who wouldn't know a rule if they saw it
– hellcats. I'm ashamed of you, Nephew. So either you'll eat
that porridge – very good for you – or go without luncheon.'

'Pooh! I'm not hungry.'

'And another thing, lad. Where's that girl Ninette gone
to – eh? *He-he-he!* Couldn't find her this morning, could you?'

'So it was you, Uncle,' Malgrim began angrily.

'You know that big flock o' geese just below the castle?
He-he-he! Now she's one o' them.'

Malgrim, who had sat down, jumped up again now. 'Why,
you unscrupulous old – '

'Sit down, lad. There's two or three hundred geese there
– you'd be all day on it. I'll turn her back as soon as we've
finished our business. And of course when you've given me a
hand with the Dimmock-dragon transformation.'

'Ha-ha! You've remembered that, have you? Awkward, isn't
it?'

'It wouldn't have been, lad, if you hadn't interfered last
night. Now King Meliot, just because Melicent wasn't there
last night, is turning nasty – says he's no proof that Sam did
kill the dragon. All your fault. Well, we'll have to attend to

Dimmock or we can't get on with our business. Sam an' Cap'n Plunket are on their way here now.'

'Are they? How do you know?'

'How do I know? I'm an enchanter, aren't I, lad? Ay – an' a better one than you. Though of course if you have an enchanter son or nephew, you'll be better than him. Just remember, lad, ours is a profession of wise men. So we have regress instead of progress. That means that as we grow old we're always the best men in our profession. And quite right too.'

'But do you see what that means?' said Malgrim earnestly. 'Why, at that rate – with steady regress – in a few hundred years – '

'They'll be no better than amateurs,' said Marlagram. 'By that time people won't believe what we could do. Can't be helped. That's regress. Come in, come in,' he called. Then, as Sam and Plunket entered: 'Sit down, sit down. What'll you take to drink?'

'Two large Malmseys,' said Plunket.

Marlagram stared at the space above the table. 'Two large Malmseys – sharp.'

The wine appeared immediately. 'Service,' said Plunket appreciatively. 'Couldn't manage a cigar, could you, old boy?'

'Not here,' said Marlagram, 'not now. Not for hundreds and hundreds of years.'

'Pity. Well – happy days!' After he had swallowed most of his wine, he went on, 'Now, Sam old boy, tell 'em.'

'Look here,' said Sam, 'you've simply got to disenchant Dimmock, and make the King believe I knocked off that dragon. And, after all, I didn't know the dragon was Dimmock when I went to challenge him. I'm not entirely a fraud.'

'Certainly not,' said Plunket. 'Who'd have thought that was Dimmock – a thing that looked like the Flying Scot with scales and knobs on? I say, Sam behaved like a hero – so he *is* a hero. But he won't be if that dragon hangs about dictating letters to his secretary.'

'You needn't argue with me,' said Marlagram. 'I want to get on with company business, the way we agreed to. So I want Dimmock here and no dragon, just as much as you two do. But it's all a bit tricky – ' He hesitated.

'Gentlemen,' said Malgrim in his grandest manner, 'I'll explain what it is my uncle shrinks from admitting. He can't restore Dimmock to his usual shape without my help.'

'If I'd time I could.'

'Possibly. Possibly not. But you haven't time, my dear Uncle.'

'That's true,' said Sam. 'That dragon ought to have gone now.'

'And you can only have my help on my terms,' Malgrim continued smoothly. 'A seat on the board of the new company. Then, Uncle, you take Ninette out of that flock of geese.'

'If that's where she is,' said Sam, 'it serves her right. You and Ninette! Miss Nutty Cake Mix of 1961! Why?'

'Pure mischief, I must confess,' Malgrim told him. 'And it made an amusing change from real life. Anyhow, those are my terms, gentlemen.'

Sam looked appealingly across the table. 'Master Marlagram, please – '

But before he could say anything else, Melicent was there, arriving so quickly that it looked as if magic had been at work.

'Master Marlagram,' she began, 'you've been helping us, and we're grateful – but don't spoil it now.'

'Here, just a minute,' said Marlagram anxiously. 'How did you get in here?'

'Exactly what I was about to ask,' said Malgrim. 'You didn't do this by yourself.'

'Nobody could, without our permission. After all, we are enchanters.'

'So who did it?'

Melicent smiled at them. 'Well, if you must know, a second cousin of mine has just arrived at the castle – and she's a girl who was taught by Morgan le Fay.'

'*What?*' Marlagram and Malgrim jumped up together, then went into an urgent huddle.

'Nephew, we're having no young sorceresses here – '

'At the last conference in Avalon, we were definitely allotted this territory – '

'But you know what women are, lad. Look, we must clear up here – Dimmock, dragon, company business an' all – '

'Right, Uncle. And then we'll see who's working the magic round here – '

'Excuse us. Now, lad – one, two, three – ' And they vanished.

Melicent laughed as she sat down. 'I thought that would set them off. There isn't any second cousin who's been with Morgan le Fay. I walked straight in here. I think the invisible demon who looks after them is sulking about something. Wasn't I clever, Sam darling?'

'Yes, you were, Melicent darling,' said Sam, still rather dazed.

'Fact is, old boy – and this is where you want to watch it – ' said Plunket, 'they're all sorceresses when they want to be. I think I'll try this invisible demon.' He stared hard at a point about three feet above the table, and then, with an air of command, said, 'I'll have another large Malmsey.'

A flagonful of wine descended on his head. There was ghostly laughter from above, in which Melicent joined as Plunket spluttered and fumed. Then Melicent looked solemnly at Sam.

'Darling, as soon as this dragon business is settled and Father has come round again, we must decide where the wedding ought to be – and then of course what I ought to wear.'

'You'll have to decide what you're going to wear,' Sam told her.

'Don't worry, darling. I intend to.'

'As for the wedding,' Sam went on, 'I think it ought to be mixed. I mean to say, both worlds are getting rather mixed now, so both worlds ought to be in it.'

'Dead right, old boy,' said Plunket, who had now finished mopping himself. 'Help the company too.'

'What company?' Melicent asked.

'Just business, my dear. Leave it to us.'

The room darkened and wobbled for a moment, and then the enchanters were back, rather out of breath but smiling.

'Nice bit o' fast work. *He-he-he!* Dimmock'll be here in a minute. We've left a dragon's head for King Meliot to inspect. He'll come round now, Sam. We've fixed that too. *He-he-he!*'

'Then I might as well tell you,' said Melicent, 'there isn't a girl sorceress at the castle. I was only teasing you. What's the matter? Why are you looking at me as if my nose were too shiny?'

Marlagram chuckled. 'You were only a day out, though. There's a young sorceress arriving tomorrow.'

'She's seen Sam in a magic mirror,' said Malgrim pointedly.

'*What?*' Melicent was horrified. She took Sam's arm posses-sively. 'Then he won't be there. But *I* will – and if she thinks she's coming here – '

But she was interrupted by the entrance of Dimmock, out of breath and looking hot and flustered. 'Sorry – Princess Melicent, gentlemen – but what with suddenly not being a dragon – and then being shot here out of that wood – I can tell you – '

'Let's go, Sam darling,' said Melicent. 'You can speak to Father, then we can decide about the wedding.' She took him out.

'Well, gentlemen,' said Dimmock, sitting down, 'before we get down to business, I must tell you I could do with a drink.'

'Certainly,' said Marlagram. 'Now then – '

'Hold it,' said Plunket. 'I'm against this invisible demon service. Isn't working well. Isn't there any other way?'

'Why not?' said Malgrim. He clapped his hands.

'Yes?' said the barmaid as she came in. 'What'll it be?'

'This is more like it,' said Plunket. 'Two large whiskies, Queenie.'

'Two large whiskies. Turned out nice again, hasn't it?'

'With all due respect,' Plunket said as the barmaid went out, 'I think this enchanter business can be overdone. Cut out the invisible domestic demon, I'd say. No magic out of hours, I'd suggest. Stick to Queenie.'

'That's magic too,' said Malgrim casually. 'She believes she's in the Private Bar of the Black Horse, waiting for opening time and day-dreaming. Perhaps she is too.'

'Perhaps we all are, old boy,' said Plunket. 'Makes you think, doesn't it?'

'No,' said Marlagram. 'Put 'em down,' he told the barmaid, who had arrived with the whiskies, 'and pop off.'

As soon as she had popped off, Dimmock asked, 'Who's in the chair?'

'I am,' said Marlagram. '*He-he-he!* Senior man present.'

'Very well,' said Malgrim. 'Now, Mr Chairman, here are my proposals. Messrs Marlagram and Malgrim to be invited to join the board of the new company, taking over from Wallaby, Dimmock, Paly and Tooks. Wallaby and Tooks to resign and their voting stock transferred to Marlagram and Malgrim. The new company to be known as Marlagram, Malgrim, Dimmock and Paly – '

'No, Mr Chairman,' said Dimmock with some heat, 'I'll accept your seniority, but I'm too well known in the advertising world to follow Mr Malgrim, for all his exceptional ability. I propose that the new agency should be known as Marlagram, Dimmock, Malgrim and Paly.'

'I'll accept that,' said Marlagram, 'so no need to vote on it – *he-he-he!* Now we want Cap'n Plunket to be general man-

ager of the subsidiary tourist agency company, to be called
Marlagram, Malgrim and Dimmock – agreed?'

'Agreed,' said Dimmock. 'But how did you know?'

'After all,' said Malgrim, 'we *are* enchanters.'

'Yes,' said Plunket, 'and it's going to be tricky running a
decent expense account with you chaps.'

'Now then, gentlemen.' Old Marlagram was very brisk.
'We split fifty-fifty on all English and Peradore business. But I
take seventy-five per cent of anything from Scotland and the
Orkneys. I've a good connection up there.'

Malgrim was equally brisk. 'And I want at least sixty-five
per cent on everything from Wales and Lyonesse.'

'There isn't such a place,' Dimmock objected.

'There is *now* – and *here*.'

'It's going to take some selling at our end.'

'On the contrary,' said Malgrim. 'To visit a place that's
vanished – what could be more attractive?'

'Quite right,' said Plunket. 'A three-day visit to Lyonesse –
full board and all excursions – bingo!'

'Chair, chair, gentlemen,' cried Marlagram. 'Now where
are we? What's the next business?'

'Mr Chairman,' said Dimmock, 'I'll tell you quite frankly,
I'm not at my best on these occasions without a cigar.'

'No use, old boy,' said Plunket, 'I've tried. Not for hundreds
and hundreds of years – '

'Don't tell me a couple of first-class enchanters working
together couldn't find us some cigars.' Dimmock looked at
them.

'Well, let's see,' said Marlagram indulgently. 'Ready,
Nephew? Quiet, you two.' The enchanters closed their eyes
and appeared to be muttering something. A few moments
later, two rather small black cigars fell on the table.

'Brazilian,' said Plunket, examining his cigar. 'I've had
better and I've had worse. Got a light, old boy?'

The room was soon thick with smoke and business.

CHAPTER SEVENTEEN

At the Wedding Feast

The feast celebrating the wedding of Sam and Melicent was probably the trickiest piece of enchantment ever attempted, so difficult that even Marlagram and Malgrim working in close alliance had to appeal for help to Morgan le Fay. The two worlds had to be brought together and joined up, for at least three hours. What began as Dimmock's office ended as the banqueting hall of King Meliot's castle. An immense table, magically constructed, went through from one world to the other. At the modern end, it was all rather sparse and severe, with guests, waiters and waitresses in black-and-white, and very little on the table; whereas at the Peradore end the table could not be seen for boars' heads, roasted peacocks and swans, barons of beef, almond-and-honey castles, flagons and tankards, and the diners there and even their serving men and maids looked equally magnificent and opulent. While the rosy Peradore servitors poured out gallons of wine and ale, laughing away at any jokes they overheard, in the modern half a melancholy waiter and a tired drawn-faced waitress, with obvious distaste, gingerly filled tiny glasses with something pale. This sharp difference had been anticipated by the Old Skipper, Cap'n Plunket, who had wangled an invitation to sit in the Peradore half for himself and Anne Dutton-Swift. The bride, in white samite, looked as beautiful as a princess in a fairy tale, which is what she was. Sam looked bewildered, as if he could not understand even yet what was happening. King Meliot looked fuddled but good-naturedly so, and he kept smiling at people he did not know who were obviously not properly dressed.

Dimmock, clutching a great many typed sheets, was proposing a toast to Peradore, and had been doing it for the last twenty minutes. It is not easy to be desperate and rambling at the same time, but that is the effect Dimmock as a toast-proposer achieved, partly because the typed sheets were never in proper order but also because he was frequently interrupted by pneumatic drills.

'And – er – concluding these brief remarks – for of course I had no idea I would be – er – called upon tonight – er – to propose this toast – finally – er – I wish to assure all our friends from Peradore' – here Dimmock shuffled the typed sheets again – 'that if – er – at any time – they wish to pay us a visit – we on our side will be only too happy – er – to show them all we can – er – to explain as best we can all those – er – amazing developments which have made for – er – progress – and – er – the triumph of – er – our great modern civilization. Let me then – '

But the pneumatic drills, which seemed to have had reinforcements, started up again. Dimmock flung down his notes in disgust, then flung himself into his chair. The drills immediately stopped. He grabbed his sheets, rose again, but the drills started. He sat down, defeated, and the drills were silent.

'Master Marlagram,' said King Meliot, 'will reply for Peradore.'

The old enchanter shot up as if he had been a jack-in-the-box. 'Your Majesty – ladies an' gentlemen – *he-he-he!* – having listened to our friend Mr Dimmock for the last half-hour I'll be very brief indeed. If he and our friends in his world should ever tire of the progress they're making – *he-he-he!* – an' the triumphs of their civilization – and if they're ready to put up with a little peace and quiet, good food an' drink, pure air, leisurely talk, a night's real sleep, an' no radioactivity to devour the marrow in their bones, we on our side will do our humble best to entertain 'em. I-thank-you-for-the-toast-

and-the-way-in-which-you-have-received-it – blah-blah-blah
– *he-he-he!*'

Marlagram sat down, still chuckling, and while the others
were applauding, Malgrim regarded him with some dis-
favour. 'Egg and pasty on your beard,' he said severely. 'And
not a good speech. Too few points and not well made. A
disappointment, I'm afraid. No pun intended.'

'Darling, be quiet,' said Ninette. 'The King – look!'

'The health of the bride and groom,' King Meliot
announced, 'will be proposed, if he isn't too plastered, by
Captain Plunket.'

Assisted by Anne Dutton-Swift, the Old Skip rose unstead-
ily, stared hard at an untouched boar's head, then let his eyes
go goggling round the company, while he made some loud
throat-clearing noises.

'Your Majesty – Princess Melicent – Sir Sam – friends,' he
began. 'Shan't talk long as most of you seem to me definitely
pie-eyed.'

'Never,' cried the barmaid, 'never, never – hup – pardon!'

This interruption gave Plunket a chance, which he took at once, to refresh himself. Now he peered mistily in the direction of the bride and bridegroom. 'Princess an' Sam say they'll live in both our worlds. Quite ri'. Good idea. I say – *good idea*,' he repeated at the top of his voice, as if he had been challenged. He glared at nobody in particular. 'Same here. I say – *same here*. Lot of talk, seem to remember, about One World. No. No, no, no.' He shook a fist at Dimmock, Herbert Paly, Mrs Dimmock, Mrs Paly, Philip Spencer-Smith and a girl he had brought called Penelope Dill, who began giggling. 'No laughin' matter. Serious subjec'. I say – Two Worlds. So does Princess, so does Sam. Diff'rence of a day of course. One end of this table it's Wednesday an' the other end it's Tuesday. So what? Who cares? Work it properly – have two Saturdays running an' never a Monday. One time in Costa Rica I thought it was Thursday for nearly a fortnight – grew a beard an' nearly learnt to play the mandolin – tell you about it some time.' He picked up a flagon and emptied it rather noisily. 'Well, tha's about all. Wha' – toast? Qui' ri'.' He frowned and made an obvious effort to be distinct. 'Now it's time for the happy pair to wish us all long luck an' the best of life. Join toast in drinking us.'

They all stood up and drank to the bridal pair. Everybody cheered and applauded, except Penelope Dill, who giggled.

'Unaccustomed as I am to public speaking,' said Melicent smoothly, 'while thanking you for the way in which you have both proposed this toast and received it, I shall ask my husband to reply on my behalf.'

'Thank you, thank you,' said Sam, looking at one end of the table and then at the other. 'Nobody realizes better than I do that I don't deserve to have won the hand and heart of a beautiful princess. I've not been clever. I've not even been very brave. Just lucky. All I can say on my own behalf is that when the great day arrived, I knew at once, without anybody telling me, that at last it was the thirty-first of June – the glorious *Thirty-first*.'

King Meliot waited until there was silence. 'We are now to have,' he announced dubiously, 'a song with lute accompaniment by Master Lamison – "The Black Knight Hath My Heart".'

Let's go, shall we?

ALSO AVAILABLE FROM VALANCOURT BOOKS

MICHAEL ARLEN	Hell! said the Duchess
R. C. ASHBY (RUBY FERGUSON)	He Arrived at Dusk
FRANK BAKER	The Birds
WALTER BAXTER	Look Down in Mercy
CHARLES BEAUMONT	The Hunger and Other Stories
DAVID BENEDICTUS	The Fourth of June
PAUL BINDING	Harmonica's Bridegroom
CHARLES BIRKIN	The Smell of Evil
JOHN BLACKBURN	A Scent of New-Mown Hay
	Broken Boy
	Blue Octavo
	A Ring of Roses
	Children of the Night
	The Flame and the Wind
	Nothing but the Night
	Bury Him Darkly
	Our Lady of Pain
	Devil Daddy
	The Household Traitors
	The Face of the Lion
	The Cyclops Goblet
	A Beastly Business
	The Bad Penny
THOMAS BLACKBURN	A Clip of Steel
	The Feast of the Wolf
JOHN BRAINE	Room at the Top
	The Vodi
JACK CADY	The Well
MICHAEL CAMPBELL	Lord Dismiss Us
R. CHETWYND-HAYES	The Monster Club
	Looking for Something to Suck
ISABEL COLEGATE	The Blackmailer
BASIL COPPER	The Great White Space
	Necropolis
	The House of the Wolf
HUNTER DAVIES	Body Charge
JENNIFER DAWSON	The Ha-Ha
FRANK DE FELITTA	The Entity
A. E. ELLIS	The Rack
BARRY ENGLAND	Figures in a Landscape

CPSIA information can be obtained
at www.ICGtesting.com
Printed in the USA
BVHW081939140122
626235BV00003B/39

9 781941 147214